MW01251929

An Empty Tomb
Where Roses Bloom

The Story of Lataine's Ring

written by **Kerry L. Barger**

Copyright © 2011 by Kerry L. Barger

All rights reserved, including the right to reproduce this book or portions thereof in any form whatsoever. Thank you for respecting the work of this author.

Library of Congress Reg. #: TXu 1-768-875 (listed as "An American Holocaust")
An Empty Tomb Where Roses Bloom / by Kerry L. Barger - Fourth Edition
ISBN-13: 978-1470169503
ISBN-10: 1470169509

The stories in this book are based on actual events. Some names have been changed. Multiple copies of this book, or any portions thereof, for classroom use may be utilized without additional permissions of any kind. This book contains and otherwise incorporates and utilizes copyrighted material, the use of which has not been specifically authorized by the copyright owners. The use of such material for purposes such as criticism, comment, teaching, scholarship, research (and other related purposes) constitutes a 'fair use' of the copyrighted material as provided for in the US Copyright Law at Title 17 U.S.C. Section 107. If you wish to use this copyrighted material for purposes of your own that go beyond 'fair use', you must obtain permission from the copyright owner/s. If for any reason you believe that the use of your material in this book does not constitute 'fair use' (as defined by law), please notify the publisher or the author's legal representative/s immediately so that the matter can be promptly addressed.

The poem *"MEMORY BOOK"* and the other writings in the Appendix were reprinted with the written permission of Carolyn Jones Frei and William Earl Capps.

Books and proceeds from the sale of this book will be donated to the New London Museum in memory of Lataine McQuaid and all those who perished alongside her.

Other books by this author include:

High Times & Rough Rides of a Bipolar Addict
- and -
"Elohim"(Ancient Science Fiction or Biblical God?)

(Hardcover, paperback and e-book versions of all books are available.)

CONTENTS

Dedication

This book is dedicated to the memory of the hundreds of innocent children who died suddenly and unexpectedly alongside my relative, Shirley Lataine Parchman McQuaid. Her story, as told by my mother, inspired me to undertake the challenge of writing this book. I can only hope that I have done justice to her memory and to all those who were affected by the events described in the following pages.

Preface

There were many disasters in the United States before 9/11, but few that affected as many people so suddenly as the one described in this book. It is one that has stayed with an entire generation for a lifetime, and would perhaps be forgotten, except for the memories recorded herein.

In May of 2011, after ten years of hiding and evading justice, Osama Bin Laden was killed by a successful Navy SEAL team operation. The country was soon riding a wave of patriotic self-satisfaction that came from this news. A world that was dramatically changed by the terrorist attacks of September 11, 2001 is now more hopeful that humankind may ultimately be free from the threatening grip of organized terror. The generation living now will continue to carry the memory of the World Trade Center being reduced to a graveyard of rubble after being struck by hijacked airliners. This act of suicidal terrorism was instigated by Osama Bin Laden. Families who lost loved ones will take their grief and their memories of this disaster to the grave. History will record the tragic event for posterity.

During the summer of 2010, I was asked to write a book based on a screenplay about the worst public school tragedy America has ever witnessed. The author of the screenplay asked me to turn his script into a companion book for a movie that was originally scheduled to be released in 2011. Accepting the challenge, I produced the first edition of this book. Due to circumstances beyond my control, the making of that movie has been delayed. However, feeling that this milestone event demands a broader place in the portals of history, I decided to write another edition that could be published immediately, simply because the stories surrounding this tragedy beg to be told. (Additional details were offered to me after the first publication and have been included in this edition.)

The original title of this book is <u>An American Holocaust: The Story of Lataine's Ring</u>. After its public debut, some individuals found this title objectionable. Not wishing to offend in any way, and being sensitive to the feelings of those who may also feel the same, I decided to release this re-titled fourth edition. It has been said that, "You cannot tell a book by its cover." However, it would not benefit an author to retain a book title that detracts from the intended message or focus of the material. After struggling with numerous alternatives, I decided on the title, <u>An Empty Tomb Where Roses Bloom</u>, hoping that readers will find it appropriate and poignant on multiple levels related to this book's content.

The individuals whose lives were extinguished in New London, Texas on March 18, 1937 have become but a footnote in history. It is my hope that this book will in some measure bring their stories forward into our own time, so that today's generation may learn from their sacrifice.

It has almost been seventy-five years since the disaster described in the following pages. No, it was not a terrorist attack, an act of war, or a genocidal massacre. It was a consequence of ignorance by well-meaning people. There remains no shortage of that commodity.

The Days Before

1. Remembering Lataine

Have you ever wondered why that pressurized fuel that fills the gas pipes in your house has an odor like rotten eggs? I used to think it was the smelly fumes of dead prehistoric animals buried deep underground whose lives were sacrificed eons ago so we can have oil and natural gas. I was wrong.

When I was just three or four and barely old enough to get into serious trouble, I asked my mother one day if she would let me light the gas heater that I had seen her light so many times. I always smelled that awful stench immediately after a gas valve was turned on. I'm not sure how many times I begged before eventually being allowed to do the honors and light it on my own. One day I asked why it stank so badly and was surprised by the answer. I was told they intentionally put that awful smell into natural gas so people would know when they have a gas leak, since gas leaks can be very dangerous. I suppose my childhood curiosity about the matter was satisfied at the time, but as I grew older, I sometimes wondered if there might be more to the story. There was. Fifty years or more would pass before I got the full story about that awful, smelly odor.

At the time of my enlightenment on this subject, my daughter and I were sitting in my mother's living room looking through my late grandmother Clemmie's tattered old family Bible. We came across Granny's handwritten entries in the family history section and were reading some of the names, dates and places denoting when and where family members were born. My daughter asked my mother, "Mimi, do you remember anything about living in New London where you were born?"

There was a stunned silence as tears filled my mother's eyes. She left the room and returned with a small jewelry box clutched in her hand. What followed was the story of a tragedy that had personally haunted and dramatically affected her and her family when she was a young child.

Mother was born in New London, Texas in 1933. Her father, my grandfather Papa Dee, worked for Humble Oil, which later became Exxon. During the first week of February in 1937, he was transferred from New London to Talco, Texas where oil had been discovered the previous year. Talco is about ninety miles from New London, as the crow flies. That was a good two to three hour drive back then, depending on the weather.

Mother's immediate family had many close friends and relatives in New London. One of those relatives was Winona McQuaid, Granny's first cousin. She and her husband had a daughter named Lataine and twin baby boys named Gale and Dale.

Mother told us that Lataine had been her playmate

when they were youngsters. She described her as a very pretty girl and remembered her having long, thick curls in her hair at one time that reminded her of Shirley Temple. They used to play together for hours, and Mother said she remembered how much she loved Lataine.

Less than two months before Mother's family moved from New London to Talco, they went shopping at the local five-and-dime. Mother told us that whenever anyone left the house the family always went together, except when Papa Dee went to work. That day they went shopping for a few Christmas gifts. Locked under a glass case was a small gold ring which had a tiny gold-leaf rose where a precious stone is normally set. Mother became fascinated with it and decided it was what she wanted to give Lataine for Christmas. It then became a tough sell, because Papa Dee hadn't planned on spending that much money. When Mother offered to give up two of the things she had on her own Christmas wish list, the sentiment was enough to persuade her parents to buy it. Mother said that when she gave the ring to Lataine, she told her it was the kind that only a princess could wear. Lataine liked her new ring so much that she swore she would wear it every day. She had no way of knowing how that ring and her father's job would eventually affect her and her family.

2. The Texas Oil Boom

Like Papa Dee, Lataine's daddy worked in the oil fields around New London, which was one of many small, laid back, oilfield boom towns in Texas. It lies 30 miles southeast of Tyler, the home of the annual Texas Rose Festival. Most of the people who lived there felt very fortunate, because they lived in one of the richest communities in the country. Local oil revenues were used to build the most modern schools and to improve education for their children. The area also provided jobs that put food on workers' tables, clothes on their backs and roofs over their heads. For the oil companies operating in the area, the mid-1930's was their heyday.

The oil industry has always been both a boon and a scourge to those communities where oil and natural gas have been discovered. Captain Anthony Lucas brought in the first major well in Texas on January 10, 1901 (the year Papa Dee was born). The well was named Spindletop after a salt dome outside of Beaumont where it was drilled. When it came gushing in, the well shot oil several hundred feet into the air and flowed at a rate of 100,000 barrels a day. At the time, that was more than all the other oil wells in the United States combined. Needless to say, it wasn't long until several large companies were formed, and oil and gas became two of the most important commodities in the country. Two of these companies were Gulf Oil and Humble Oil, which later became Exxon.

Wherever there was oil and gas to be found, laborers were needed in abundance. The *roughnecks* who worked in the Texas oil fields were incredibly tough, and the jobs were downright nasty. I know this from personal experience, having financed a portion of my college education from summer work in the oilfields around Luling on a roustabout crew. The first thing I needed every evening when I got home after work was a thorough scrubbing and clean clothes.

The men who worked in the oilfields during the Texas "boom town" years in the first half of the last century soon became known as *oilfield trash* by those who didn't favor their sudden appearance by the hundreds into their formerly quiet rural communities. Places never known for any sort of night life often spawned dozens of new honky-tonks, raucous and rowdy dance halls, and infrequent fistfights that sometimes got out of hand and necessitated intervention by local law enforcement officials.

As I mentioned previously, oilfield workers were typically covered from head to toe in oil, grease, dirt and grime after a day's work. Wives and mothers often had to soak an oil man's filthy clothes in kerosene or gasoline to loosen the oil before washing. Because this created volatile gas fumes, the practice also began causing the occasional explosion in homes when families started using electric and gas heated clothes dryers in the 1930's, instead of simply hanging their clothes outside to dry. A growing demand for safer, more powerful laundry detergents also resulted in competitive advertising on popular daytime radio programs that targeted stay-at-home wives, thus the term "soap opera" was born.

Those parents who referred to oilfield workers as *trash* did not want their teenage daughters dating or marrying them. Some young women lied about their age in order to marry the men of their choice. Mother told us that since my Papa Dee was considered by Granny's daddy to be one of these men, he and Granny had to wait until she became 18 and of legal age to marry him.

Papa Dee had been working in the oilfields since boom towns began sprouting up in all sorts of places all over Texas in the 1920's. Before that, Mother said he drove a team of mules with his brothers wherever they could find work building roads in Texas and Oklahoma. Granny and Papa Dee had both picked cotton growing up. Granny started picking cotton at the age of seven, along with her older brothers, to help support their family. Granny always blamed her mild scoliosis on having to pick cotton as a child.

During his teen years, Papa Dee had suffered with

typhoid fever. Granny always kept a photo of Papa Dee from when he was sick and had lost all his hair. He was unable to walk for almost a year, but survived (unlike so many others who were stricken with the same disease).

Papa Dee and Granny's first child, my Uncle Gerald, was born in 1926. Their second child, Mildred, died at age three with scarlet fever in 1931. The entire family was quarantined because of the scarlet fever and was not permitted to attend her funeral. All they got to see were some photos that were taken by other family members at Mildred's graveside service.

Mother told us that less than a handful of the men in our extended family did any good at all in the oil business. Most went broke and stayed that way or gambled away every dollar they earned except for what they spent on liquor. A few, like Papa Dee, simply worked a steady job and tried to keep their families intact. Unlike so many others during the difficult economic times of the 1930's, they somehow managed to keep working and make ends meet. Often they helped support their brothers and sisters, along with their aging parents. Decent jobs were hard to find. Today's newscasts present a similar picture in the American job market, as thousands of decent families suffer similar unemployment woes and any savings they have soon dries up.

When I was a child, Papa Dee told me he had saved

$50 a month from every paycheck he ever earned. It doesn't sound like much now, but that was much more than 10% of his salary back then. That money got his family through their toughest times, and what was left eventually allowed him to retire when the time came.

Because of frequent transfers, oilfield work was not typically the kind of career choice that brought families closer together for very long, except when tragedy struck. It would strike hard in East Texas in 1937.

The East Texas oilfield is still the largest and most prolific oil reservoir in the contiguous United States and sits on the northwestern corner of the state's Piney Woods region. Most of the drilling for oil and natural gas started in Texas as wildcat drilling. A "wildcat" well is always a speculative venture in any spot not known to be productive, but this area was the most productive in the state and such speculation usually paid off. Wildcat drilling is a very expensive way to gamble. The odds of striking oil or gas are mostly slim to none without first doing extensive seismological testing in order to find a good drilling site. Such technology was not yet widely in use at the time, but drilling a deep hole just about anywhere around New London left any experienced speculator or drilling company with a fairly good chance of hitting pay dirt.

Since the discovery of the East Texas oilfield in 1930 near present-day New London, over 30,000 wells have since been drilled within its 140,000 acres that spreads across five Texas counties. At the end of 1933, the East Texas field reported its greatest production year, pumping out of the ground over 216 million barrels of oil and nearly eight billion cubic feet of natural gas. During 1936, crude oil prices remained steady, selling at $1.05 per barrel. Today's prices are approaching a hundred times that, which probably says more about the value of the American dollar than the value of forty-two gallons of crude. Around the beginning of 1937, prices spiked to an average of $1.17 per barrel... an all-time high! Immediately following that price hike, Mexico officially nationalized its oil production and reserves on March 2nd, 1937. That move has never been favored by American oil investors north of the border and served to increase international tension between the U.S. and Mexico.

To maximize profits and minimize losses, the large oil companies that moved into the East Texas area soon learned to streamline their drilling operations. Once an initial well had been drilled to a safe depth, the drilling rig was moved off the site and a less expensive service rig that was specifically built for the last phase of the drilling process would be moved in to bring in the well and get it up and running. This freed up the primary drilling rig to begin drilling another hole without risking the most expensive operating equipment and also improved the efficiency of large-scale operations. Lataine's daddy, J. W. "Jake" McQuaid supervised one of these dangerous service rigs.

Wednesday
March 17, 1937

3. A Wildcat Well

Jake McQuaid had reported to work as usual on this particular day. At the end of February, Jake and his crew had moved their service rig and started completion drilling on a well that was situated near the city limits. It had been so cold when Jake first began drilling in this location, that the euphemistic expression "colder than a well-digger's butt" came home to roost for him and his men. I remember Papa Dee using that expression often after coming in from his job in the oilfields on cold winter days. I've heard it said that Texas really only has two seasons: summer and winter. For the most part, I've found that to be true, in that it is typically uncomfortably cold or simply too hot to keep folks from complaining about the weather.

Now that the first official day of spring was half a week away, the Texas sun was beating down strongly enough to soak the shirts of the men working in the East Texas oilfields with perspiration. The heat also caused watermarks to darken around the western style felt hats that were worn by most oilfield workers when they didn't have to wear a metal hardhat. Shirts were beginning to come off in the mid-day heat, and the water coolers sitting on the sides of work trucks began demanding a daily trip to the local icehouse before the evening shift started.

This Saint Patrick's Day arrived just six weeks after

Papa Dee and Granny had moved from New London to Talco with their children. It was also the same day Amelia Earhart left California in 1937 to begin her first attempt at a record-breaking airplane flight around the world. She set a new speed record and would be greeted in Hawaii wearing a traditional lei, amid a crowd of reporters and photographers. This would also become an earth-shaking day for Lataine's daddy and his work crew.

Jake McQuaid was a big man of around six feet, but he could scale to the top of any oil derrick in record time and get back to the ground even quicker. One of his roughnecks had walked off the job the first week of March because of a dispute over money that he owed one of the other workers. That argument almost led to both men getting canned. Jake was a military veteran and would not tolerate any monkey business from his men, although I can't say that he ever spoke about his life in the military. Even so, every worker he supervised knew that if a situation got out of hand and fists were thrown, either one or both men were going to be fired on the spot.

Jake had recently been assigned a new greenhorn, Buster Nugent, as a replacement on the evening shift, but he had not yet figured out whether this twenty-one year old kid had enough sense to work on the rig without getting himself or someone else hurt or killed. So far, Buster had been given general maintenance duties that didn't require any special skills, but that was about to change.

After his first day on the job, Buster had written to his mom and told her, *I've been burying dead men and painting Christmas trees all day!* The next day he wrote her again and explained that "dead men" were the heavy stays they bury to steady the derricks and that "Christmas trees" were the pipes and fittings in the center of the well. His mom was relieved when she got his second letter, but she also knew the time would soon come for Buster to begin earning his pay as a roughneck and that the dangers were very real.

Jake's workday was going pretty much like any other. After an uneventful morning and having finished his sack lunch, he decided it was a good afternoon to train his newest derrick hand to work the crow's nest located 110 feet above ground at the top of the derrick. Buster had reported for work almost an hour early, near the end of Jake's lunch hour. He soon got his new assignment for the day.

"Get on up that ladder, Buster. It's time you got used to the high life!" Jake always believed there was no time like the present to get things done.

Buster wasn't amused by Jake's cavalier order for him to climb the derrick ladder, but he swallowed his pride, placed both his feet on the bottom rung, took a deep breath and began the climb. Buster wasn't afraid of heights, but the tallest structure he had ever worked on before was a two-story house where he had done a roofing job. He had been reporting for work on time everyday since he started working for Jake and was ready to learn whatever he could, even before his shift began.

Because of their success in the oil business around New London, Humble had built a bunkhouse and a mess hall in the Humble Camp where the newest employees like Buster were staying and taking their meals. Buster had grown up seeing too many families living from paycheck to paycheck and decided that was not for him. Recognizing that real money was to be made in the oil business, Buster was determined to make a name for himself. He was also smart enough to know he had to learn the business from the ground up and that Jake McQuaid was the man to teach him.

From what I was told, Buster got about fifteen feet above the ground and was reaching for the next rung on the ladder when Jake's voice bellowed out, "Where in God's name do you think you're going like that? …straight to hell more than likely! Get your butt back down here!"

Buster could tell Jake was serious. He immediately climbed back down and asked, "What's wrong, Boss?"

"Where you from, Cowboy?" asked Jake sternly.

"Oklahoma, Sir." Buster responded as if he was a

fresh military recruit in basic training.

"Don't they have ladders up there in that backwoods part of North Texas?" Although originally from Illinois, Jake had become as proud of living and working in Texas as most natives.

Buster looked at his boss quizzically. "What am I doing wrong, Mr. McQuaid?"

Jake calmed himself and explained, "When I looked up and saw you climbing that ladder like a monkey, it took me back to when I first started in this business. If you look at any old derrick that's been standing for awhile, you'll see rungs missin' from the ladder. We've got a fairly new derrick here, but you never know when that first rung is going to break. They break off close to the ground, in the middle and sometimes a hundred feet up. Anytime a rung breaks under your foot, it'll scare the living daylights out of you, but it won't kill you if you know what you're doing. You obviously don't! I can't tell you how many times that's happened to me and my boys here. If you're holding on to one when it breaks, you're liable to fall and break your stupid neck! I'm only gonna tell you this once. If I ever see you climb a ladder like that again, it will be the last day you work for me! Keep both of your hands on the side of the rails when you're climbing up and coming down and never rest both your feet at the same time on the same rung. You got that, Boy?"

"Yes, sir. It'll never happen again." Buster soon realized that Jake was just looking after him, and that he did indeed have a lot to learn. The other men on the platform couldn't help but overhear Jake chewing on the new greenhorn. They just grinned at each other wide-eyed and shook their heads, recalling similar words when they first started working for Jake McQuaid.

After relaxing his serious stare through the eyes of the younger Buster Nugent, Jake looked around briefly to notice the other men who were watching him and waiting to see what would happen next. I can't say whether or not this bunch would later become a ship of fools, but there was no mistaking who the captain was on that day.

Accepting that the fresh recruit had learned his first valuable lesson of the day, Jake softened his tone and said, "OK, Son. Let's try this again. I'll follow you up when you get settled in the nest." Jake walked across the platform and started laughing with his other men while they all watched Buster ascend over 100 feet into the air.

My first experience of having a ladder rung break off in my hands was when I was about eleven and had climbed about fifty feet up a water tower just for the fun of it. That could well have been the end of me and my cousin below me, but for luck and childhood agility. Buster assumed that his boss was worried about him falling down on top of him. Jake, however, wasn't concerned. The thought of facing death seems to have a lasting effect on people. He knew that Buster would never climb another ladder by holding on to the rungs. It wasn't because Buster was as green as a St. Patty's Day parade that Jake didn't follow immediately. He never followed any man up a ladder.

By the time Jake's evening shift workers reported for duty and relieved the morning shift crew, Jake and Buster were ready to begin working with the drill pipes at the top of the derrick. Jake ordered the rig to be fired up. The drilling process commenced and would continue uninterrupted into the late afternoon.

4. *The London School*

When he was at the top of the derrick, Jake could see his daughter's school. It was the largest building for a hundred miles in any direction. He took a small joy anticipating the sight of the blue and gold school buses that were carrying Lataine and the other students home. Sometimes he knew exactly which bus she was riding when he saw it stop in front of the Pilgreen lease where he and his family lived. As the evening shift continued their work, Jake would check his watch from time to time until he saw the last buses leaving the London School and knew that Lataine's final class had dismissed for the day.

Jake would later tell Papa Dee that while he was waiting to see her bus, he often daydreamed about what his daughter would grow up to be; perhaps a doctor who would save lives, or a lawyer to keep people honest. Maybe she would simply be a wife and mother. He didn't care, he knew he would always love and cherish her.

While Jake had been working, Lataine had been attending her fifth grade classes in the main building at the London School. Originally known as simply *London*, the town changed its name to *New London* in 1931, but the school retained its original name as the London School. It had replaced a four-room, four-teacher schoolhouse. From all I have ever read about it, everyone was very proud of the new school because it was without doubt the finest in Texas, sitting squarely in the middle of this highly productive oilfield.

Mrs. Wright's final class of the day had just begun in Room 102. The teacher started her class by announcing a change in many of the students' schedules that would take place on the following day. The dance students who would be performing for the PTA were told to report to the gym on Thursday before the last class period began. Those who were participating in the Henderson meet on Friday needed to report to the auditorium instead of their last period class. All Friday classes had been canceled so that all students could either attend or participate in the annual interscholastic meet, a scholastic and athletic competition to be hosted that year in the neighboring town of Henderson. Many of the teachers also planned to be there to coach the students who were scheduled to participate.

Over-crowding in the 5th grade had necessitated shifting that grade over to the Intermediate and High School buildings. The first four grades were held in a separate, smaller building on the London School campus. Their school day was an hour shorter, so the first bus run usually left the school around 3:00 pm carrying the youngest students. The second bus run usually left an hour or so later carrying the upper grade students. Transportation to and from the school was provided using

30-seat bus-trailers.

The school was perched atop one of the richest oil deposits in the United States and located right smack dab in the middle of the *Oil Patch* that had sprung up following the discovery of major oil deposits in Rusk County. The school property maintained seven producing oil wells on the grounds. The London School truly was one of the most modern facilities in the world and boasted educational opportunities rarely available during the Depression Era. The London Wildcats played football in the first high school stadium in the state to have electric lights. It was no coincidence that the students had chosen to call themselves the Wildcats. That name pretty much exemplified the spirit of the area's recent history.

Those who attended classes in the New London school were a privileged group of young people. Most families had come to the region because hard-working, able-bodied men found oilfield work there. There was money literally flowing out of the earth beneath their feet. The school boasted tennis courts, music programs, a marching band, University of Texas Interscholastic League preparations, a post-graduate program and educational opportunities that were not available in most other rural areas of the country.

Construction had begun on the London School in 1931 and was completed the following year at a cost of one million dollars. Today, the cost to build similar structures would run around sixteen million. The junior-senior high building alone cost $300,000. It was the main centerpiece of the campus. Its steel-framed structure was designed in a California-Spanish style, with hollow tiles and brick trimmed in stone. It was set on sloping ground, so although it appeared from the front to be a one-story structure, anyone approaching from the rear would see two stories.

The school board in New London had overridden the architect's original plans for a boiler and steam distribution system, instead opting to install gas heaters throughout the main building. A large dead-air space beneath the structure ran the entire 253-foot length of the building's facade and was fifty-six feet wide. It was accessed through crawlspace doors in the basement and was sometimes used for storage. The basement was at ground level on the backside of the building.

Each successive year more amenities were added to the facilities. By the end of 1936, the main campus included a modern gymnasium, industrial arts facilities, an auditorium, agricultural building, sewing centers, stenography rooms, a chemistry department, and even a classical music center.

In January of 1937 the school board, with the knowledge and approval of Superintendent W. C. Shaw, canceled their natural gas contract with United Gas Company to save $300 a month, because Parade Gasoline Company offered to donate their "green" gas to the school. The school had their plumbers install a tap into Parade's residue gas line at a wellhead on the premises. This money-saving practice had become widespread and was commonly accepted for homes, schools, and churches in the Texas oilfields. It was also viewed as an environmentally friendly recycling effort, since the odorless natural gas residue that accumulated during the gasoline extraction process was otherwise considered a waste product and flared off. Student life at the London School was about as good as it got for children of working class families in the 1930's! At least that's what everyone believed.

On this particular St. Patrick's Day, the children were getting somewhat restless as the day wore on, and it was extremely warm inside the classroom. Mrs. Wright always tried to refocus her students' attention away from the playful interactions that typically accompanied the start of their last class of the day by introducing something that would interest them. She noticed Billy reach over to Ollie and give him a slight pinch on the arm while chiding the shy youngster because he wasn't wearing something green. Some of the others started to chuckle and imitate Billy's antics. Mrs. Wright stood to address her class.

"Can anyone tell me why we celebrate Saint Patrick's Day every year?" asked Mrs. Wright.

Sybil raised her hand, and the teacher called her name. "Because he drove the snakes out of Ireland?"

Never wasting an opportunity to be the center of attention, Billy blurted out, "I sure would like to get him over to our place. We've got the biggest snakes in the county around my daddy's barn!"

The other children couldn't hold back their laughter. Mrs. Wright betrayed a smile at the corner of her lips, then instructed the students near the windows to open them wider to allow a bit more fresh air to circulate in the room.

The marching Wildcat High School Band had just begun their practice for the day out on the football field. The breeze felt warm and humid coming out of the southeast, but it was still cooler than the air in the room. The children hardly noticed the sound of the oil wells pumping on the school property, but the steady banging of the big bass drum and the high notes of clarinets and cymbals filled the air in the room with the sounds of a typical afternoon at school.

Some of the students in the classroom were wearing green paper cutouts of a three-leaf clover on their shirts that they had made in an earlier class that day. There were also cardboard cutouts of leprechauns, shamrocks and even pots of gold shining with glitter posted around on the walls of the classroom.

Glenn was staring listlessly out the window, gazing at a field of Texas bluebonnets across the open school grounds. Like most of the boys his age, he wore blue denim overalls to class. During the previous summer, Glenn had picked cotton for landowner and bus driver Lonnie Barber, alongside his friend Joe Bo, who was in his fifth grade English class down the hall. Glenn and Joe Bo made a nickel an hour picking cotton. That was a worthy minimum wage for boys their age during the Depression. The boys worked in Mr. Barber's cotton fields filling bags from sunup to sundown. Both knew what it was like to come home exhausted with filthy hands and fingernails and a sore back.

Glenn reached into his shirt pocket and pulled out one of those green paper shamrocks and a small safety pin. He reached forward and touched Lataine's light brown hair that was streaked with gold from her time in the Texas sun. Her morning curls had fallen in the moist heat of the afternoon, partially covering the thin straps on her shoulders. She turned her head and smiled. He handed her the three-leaf clover he had made earlier in the day. She gracefully accepted it and pinned it to her yellow gingham dress that was almost touching the floor. Neither spoke a word. There was no need. The classroom's activities were the last thing on their minds. Their thoughts had already drifted out the window toward the end of the school day. They were eager to get home, join their friends, and play in the afternoon sun. Both could feel the peace that comes with believing there is plenty of time for everything.

Their daydreaming was interrupted by Mrs. Wright's voice. "Before we get into today's lesson, your homework assignment for tomorrow is to trace the outline of Texas from the map on page 22 that divides the state into different regions. Then indicate on your map what natural resources are found in each region and be prepared to answer the questions at the end of Chapter 12 in class tomorrow."

The students opened their geography books and began turning pages. A few disgruntled sighs were heard as the students tried to find the map their teacher had indicated.

Mrs. Wright continued, "Joyce, please read your answer to question number one at the end of Chapter 11 from today's assignment."

Joyce found her homework from the night before, still folded in her book, and began to read over the recognizable strains of their school's Alma Mater. The band music was coming from behind the gym, which sat a hundred feet from the main building. Ever-present were muffled sounds of the pumping oil wells on the school property. Apparently, there was not even one person residing in or near New London who recognized the impending danger those pumping oil wells represented.

Ollie and Billy, who were best friends, planned to spend the afternoon together at Billy's house. They were fidgeting in their seats, anxiously waiting for the last bell of the day to ring.

An Empty Tomb (CS)

5. The Pond

When school let out on March 17th, Ollie rode the bus to Billy's house, where he would stay until his mom picked him up after work. Billy's grandmother gave the boys some soda crackers and fresh milk from the morning milking when they arrived. Pasteurization of milk became common in the 1930's, but many people still milked their cows by hand. Back then, folks would would separate the cream from the milk and either churn it and make butter or serve it over cereal. Mother told me she always hated churning butter, but Granny often had her help out in order to make enough to sell and earn some extra money.

Eleven-year-old Billy hadn't been lying about the snakes in his daddy's barn when he spoke out of turn in class earlier that day. During the winter months, it was not uncommon for large snakes to get between bales of hay in the barn for warmth.

While they were enjoying their milk and crackers, Billy told Ollie about an experience he'd had a few weeks before. One day his father was tending to their cattle, and Billy had wandered into the tool shed that was next to their barn. Hearing what sounded like a loud rattle, he had cautiously bent over to look behind the tools where the sound emanated. His heart leapt into his throat when a huge snake's body came into view. It appeared to him to be as big around as a tire off a Model-T Ford. He had seen what looked like a diamond pattern on its back, and ran to tell his dad there was a rattlesnake in the shed.

Sternly telling Billy to remain where he was, his dad had gone into the tool shed and returned a few minutes later carrying the dead snake. When he had hung it from the barn door, they could see it was at least six feet long, even longer than his dad was tall. His dad had informed Billy that it was only a rat snake, but that they imitated rattlers by beating their tails against anything that would make noise. There are very few rattlesnakes in this part of the country but the number of poisonous cottonmouth water moccasins, copperheads and coral snakes more than make up for it.

After their snack, the two boys decided to walk to the home of another fifth grade friend of theirs named Wayne, who lived about a quarter mile down the road. There was a huge oak tree in Wayne's front yard that the boys had enjoyed climbing on many occasions, but now they were banned from climbing it by Wayne's parents, because Wayne had fallen out of it the year before and broken an arm. Looking for something to do, the three decided to walk across the road, hop a fence and go exploring. They were each armed with a homemade slingshot composed of a forked stick with a slice of inner tube rubber tied to it on either side. The rubber was long enough to place a rock or marble in the end. They would then hold the rock or marble between two fingers, stretch the rubber and let fly.

All three boys had achieved a modicum of efficiency with their homemade weapons. Each one had knocked down an occasional bird or two. At one time, Billy had even hit a squirrel in the head with a rock, knocking it unconscious long enough for him to kill it with a stick. His dad had helped him skin it, and his grandmother had cooked it with her fried chicken. To Billy, the squirrel meat naturally tasted much better than the drumsticks he usually ate.

The previous summer, accompanied by Wayne's older brother, the boys had taken their slingshots and some marbles to a nearby pond that was full of fat bullfrogs and had brought home enough frog legs for a meal. Billy's grandmother had made the boys clean up in the water barrel before setting foot in the house, because they were covered with mud from retrieving their frogs and marbles in and around the pond. Billy's daddy had entertained the boys royally by showing them how salting the frog legs after they were in the frying pan kept them kicking over and over again.

This particular afternoon, after exploring a creek that ran between Wayne and Billy's house, the boys decided to walk to the large pond behind the barn. They had never fished or gone swimming there, even though it was the largest pond on the property. Billy had ridden his horse through it once just to see what it would be like. He had seen cowboys do that in the movies. Billy had gotten his dad's best saddle soaking wet on that particular day and thought he would be angry, but he wasn't. His daddy was an experienced horseman. He simply told Billy that, unlike in the movies, he needed to slide to the rear of the horse and hold onto its tail the next time he decided to take his horse for a swim.

Billy and Ollie loved Western movies. They particularly liked the Hopalong Cassidy movies and had seen every John Wayne and Buck Jones film they could see. They always tried to go to the theater when a new Western was showing in Overton, just four miles from New London. The theater there had been built in 1935. Every town that boasted of more than one horse soon had a movie theater on Main Street by the time *Gone with the Wind* and *The Wizard of Oz* would be released two years later in 1939. However, the only scenes being recorded on this day were ones that would play over and over in each of the boys' memories.

Upon arriving at the pond, all three stepped up onto the edge of the tall bank. The water was smooth as glass and dark green in the afternoon sun. It looked as if it was inviting them to jump in.

"I know it's deep enough to swim in. When I rode my horse through it last summer, she had to swim when she got to the middle." said Billy. "What do y'all think about goin' in?"

Neither Wayne nor Ollie was eager to get into the water. They walked all the way around the pond looking for any signs of life with their slingshots ready to fire, but saw nothing except a frog or two that jumped in the water before they could get a shot off. The pond was about 100 feet across from one bank to the other.

Billy persisted, "Come on guys! Let's go swimmin'!"

Wayne looked at Ollie and asked, "How about you, Ollie? I'll go in if you will."

Ollie hesitated, but when the other two started taking off their clothes, he joined them. All three stripped down to their underwear, but just as Wayne was ready to dive in, Billy stopped him. "Don't jump in there yet until we make sure nothing is under the water! My uncle's brother-in-law, Danny Miller, who lives way over in Sugar Hill did that and dove into a pond where he hadn't been swimmin' before. He hit his head on an oil drum that was under the water. It broke his neck and now he's paralyzed for the rest of his life. And he was older than we are!"

All three waded into the pond until it got over their heads and they had to swim. The water was cold and refreshing. They splashed around, then ran and jumped off the bank over and over again until the pond was no longer smooth, clear or green. The water in the entire pond became a thick, reddish gray. When they got out, they couldn't see through an inch of water from all the mud they had stirred up on the bottom. By the time they got back into their overalls, the water was smooth and calm again, but still muddy.

Ollie looked toward the middle of the pond and yelled, "Look over there!"

"What is it?" asked Wayne.

The boys stood and watched as Ollie pointed at the water in the pond. Billy whispered, "Now I see him..."

"There's another one!" exclaimed Wayne.

All three stood there mesmerized, staring at the pond in awe. They were barefoot and motionless, quietly frozen on the edge of the bank, watching and looking at each other as one deadly water moccasin's head after another popped up. They could feel the goose bumps on their arms as they tried to count all the venomous snakes in the water, but finally gave up and headed home. They had been oblivious to any danger or threat whatsoever and were soon feeling more fortunate than foolish.

6. Pay Dirt

While the boys had been swimming, Jake had been teaching Buster every nuance and safety protocol at the top station of the drilling operation by doing every task himself at least two or three times first and explaining to Buster what must be done and how. Before Jake left work, he wanted to make sure Buster was ready to work the crow's nest without him.

Seemingly out of the blue, he told Buster that when it got dark he wanted him to replace all the burned out bulbs that spanned the rig on all sides from top to bottom, keeping it well lit for the men working at night.

Jake knew the thought of such a task would challenge his new rookie, but he also wanted him to think about how to accomplish such a task. He planned to ask Buster how he would go about it before nightfall, so Jake could make sure he didn't try to do anything that would put his safety at risk. Jake soon started to take a liking to this kid and thought that maybe he had actually landed a "keeper".

The drill bit continued turning and grinding deeper into the earth, while the workmen below the derrick kept slinging chains, turning tongs, and adding new drill pipe at a steady pace. The rig's motor popped and growled with deafening roars. The rhythm of the men shifting and twisting steel drill pipes with their iron tools continued to echo with the ringing and squeaking sounds of metal against metal, disrupting an otherwise quiet country atmosphere as the hours passed.

Buster had been watching, learning and assisting his mentor, but he soon began to wonder how he would climb out on the derrick to get within reach of the burned-out light bulbs when night fell. He knew Jake wouldn't be there that night, and he didn't want to look stupid in front of the other men by having to ask for help. The lights were hanging on all sides of the giant derrick, making it appear from a distance like a gigantic Christmas tree at night. In the distance from the top of the derrick, Jake noticed Lataine's bus as it entered the Pilgreen lease to drop her safely back home.

Suddenly the drill pipe in the center of the tower dropped six to eight feet into the hole and the engine driving the drill bit sputtered and revved higher. They cut the power to the drill motor. The sudden silence left the men with ringing ears. Jake felt a low rumbling below his feet, then heard a loud, familiar hiss coming from the wellhead that sounded like the brakes venting on a freight train. He yelled out to the team below, "How deep are we?"

A voice echoed back, "Thirty-five hundred feet."

"Hot damn! We got us a well! Buster, get down that ladder as fast as you can, but be careful and remember what I told you!"

Jake started to order the men below him to shut off the main valve, but he could see that they had already started turning the big valve wheel to do just that. Buster climbed down the ladder, carefully holding onto the side rails. Jake tied off one end of his 125-foot safety line and tossed the other end of the line to the deck on the other side of Buster, who had just stepped off the ladder onto the platform deck. Jake looped the line through his safety belt so it would maintain just enough tension to release him, but still keep him from falling too fast. He straddled the ladder, grabbed both rails with his thick leather gloves and placed his boots on the outer side of the rail as he began to slide downward. He kept just enough tension on his safety line to come down at a steady pace. The deep rumbling had alerted Jake to the possibility of danger. He had seen wells blow out before, and his unconventional method of getting down the derrick ladder as fast as possible was no show of celebration.

When he landed safely on the platform deck, Jake went immediately to the wellhead and checked the pressure gauge at the main shutoff valve. He quickly grabbed his pen from his shirt pocket and wrote a number on the back of his hand. Then he checked his watch, looked closely again at the gauge a second time, and wrote another number below the first one.

"Do we need to step off, Boss?" asked one of his senior workers.

"Yes, Sir. I think we do." said Jake. Then he yelled out, "EVERYBODY CLEAR THIS DECK !!!"

He swiftly motioned for all the men to step off the platform, making sure Buster was ahead of him. If the well was going to blow, he wanted his men at a safe distance. Once everyone was on the ground, he moved to the front of the pack, making sure all his men were accounted for and continued marching away from the derrick.

As the group approached his work truck, Jake told Buster to grab the water cooler and follow closely. They continued walking away from the well into the open field for another fifty or sixty paces until Jake stopped his determined march, turned around and gazed up at the rig and the derrick.

"Well boys, let's get us some water and sit a spell. I'm not taking y'all back over there tonight. We don't want to be anywhere near that fresh well if the pressure in the hole blows the wellhead." He pointed in the opposite direction from their derrick and said, "Just look over yonder!"

The sun was setting in the west, but in the distance on the darkening eastern horizon they could see the glow of a blown out well that had been spewing a thirty to sixty-foot flame of ignited natural gas for several hours.

"That's one hell of a blowout!" commented one of

Jake's men. "I wonder if that's an Humble rig?"

"Can't be sure from here. I'm just hoping they're all still alive. If our well holds, we've caught ourselves a lucky break. Thanks men! Y'all make a damn fine drilling crew."

Jake took off his gloves, reached over suddenly and tipped Buster's hardhat from his head to the ground. Then he grabbed him from behind and buried his knuckles into Buster's short, curly hair while rubbing gruffly on his scalp. Buster was taken aback, pulled himself away from Jake and turned to face his boss. "That's for luck, Son! You've had one hell of a day, haven't you, Boy? Pretty soon we'll be able to get out of here and celebrate!"

The rest of the men joined in and grabbed Buster, each in turn reaching to rub on his head with a guffaw until he became agitated and started slapping at everyone who approached him and yelling for them to stop. Buster started grinning once again as the men kept on laughing. They quickly eased up when they thought he had had enough of their antics and began patting him on the back and gently shaking at his shoulder with one hand to let him know they had always had his back and were still on his side.

"You're all right, Kid!"

"It's OK, Nugent... we're just funnin' with ya'! That first day in the nest is always the toughest!"

"I bet old Jake had you worried all day about getting

to those rig lights. We'll change those out when we move this rig tomorrow."

Buster looked over at Jake, whose wide-eyed grin betrayed his mischief. Buster rolled his eyes and head back, then covered his head and face with one hand as he bent forward again, realizing full well that he'd been had.

"You earned a beer on me today, Buster!" Jake handed Buster a five dollar bill and told him to take his truck, go straight to the office and report to the project engineer that the well had come in. "On your way back, pick us up a couple of six-packs and some peanuts. But don't drink any until I give the OK. You're still on the clock."

Buster returned around sundown, and they placed the beer in the water cooler to remain unopened until the men were off-duty. Mr. Jaffe, the engineer, arrived shortly, dressed in a suit and tie. He was about fifteen years older than any of the other men. Jaffe noticed that Jake and his crew were in the open field away from the rig and joined them.

"So… you hit a pocket? What do you think it is Jake?" asked Jaffe.

Jake replied, "I heard her belching gas down below, and we're at depth. I'd be afraid to do any more over there until we let her sit overnight and make sure that wellhead is gonna hold. The hole pressure was building when I checked it. That was right before ordering the men off the rig." Then Jake reported the specific pressure gauge readings to Mr. Jaffe that were written on the back of his hand.

"In that case, assign your best man to stay out here and keep an eye on the rig. Make sure he doesn't get any closer than this until I get here in the morning. You can send the rest of your boys home for the night, Jake. Good work, men!"

Jake pointed in the direction of the flame spewing on the horizon and ask Jaffe, "Is that one of ours?"

"No, Sir. To my knowledge there's only a few independents operating over in that direction. I'm sure we'll hear about that one tomorrow. Their rig won't likely be of any use anymore."

Mr. Jaffe shook each worker's hand and patted Buster on the back saying, "Looks like your first drilling job has brought us some luck, Mr. Nugent."

Then he turned back to Jake and said, "Hell fire, Jake… we were supposed to be off duty over an hour ago. Toss me one of those cold ones from the cooler, and let's drink up, boys!"

7. Planning Tomorrows

Back at the London School, it was after quitting time for the maintenance men who were helping Lemmie Butler in the basement. Mr. Butler, the shop instructor, was twenty-eight years old and a graduate of East Texas Teacher's College in Commerce. Both he and his wife were teachers at the school. Late that afternoon, the principal, Mr. Waggoner, had assigned two maintenance staff to assist Lemmie in making new set decorations and murals for the next day's student dance presentations. They had been busy much of the afternoon sawing, nailing and painting.

The dance performances were scheduled at the beginning of the PTA meeting on the following afternoon. The PTA meeting was normally held in the auditorium, but the stage was too small for this presentation, so it was moved to the gym.

From all accounts, the individual maintenance workers served the school in multiple roles as janitors, plumbers, carpenters and general handymen... depending on whatever type of work was called for on a given day. Lemmie planned to do everything he could this afternoon and have his students finish the work on any remaining stage props the following morning. He would then make sure any final touches were made and that everything would be ready before the last class of the day when the PTA meeting was scheduled.

The younger of the two maintenance men plugged in the industrial table sander and began to smooth the rough edges on one of the new wooden stage props. Having to yell over the noise of the machine, he remarked, "Boy, Howdy! This thing really makes the sparks fly when you hit a nail. HOW DO YOU TURN IT OFF ???"

Lemmie could barely make out what he was saying over the noise and simply yelled back for him to unplug it. He unplugged the cord from the wall socket and left it the way he had found it.

The senior maintenance man commented, "I'm plum tuckered out… let's go home and get supper. We can finish up the rest of this stuff tomorrow." Lemmie made a mental note of their progress in order to remember what work still needed to be completed, then agreed it was time to go home for the night.

They shut off the lights and were on their way out when they were met by the night watchman who was there to investigate the noises coming from the basement. There was generally no one working in the main building this late in the evening.

"Hey boys… what was all that racket coming from down here?" The night watchman was William Crawford McClelland. He went by Will, but some called him Mr.

Mac.

The head maintenance worker greeted the night watchman with a handshake. "Hello, Will. You must've heard us using the shop equipment. My boy here got carried away testing out some of the power tools."

Embarrassed by the remark, the younger worker looked down while reaching up to adjust his cap that was now covered with sawdust.

"We'll have to get back down there again tomorrow and finish up the job, but it shouldn't take long. The sun's about to set. I reckon you just came on duty?" observed Lemmie.

"Yes, sir." answered Mr. Mac. "I'm hopin' to have a quiet night from here on out."

Lemmie replied, "I hope we both do. I truly do. Anyhow, we're beat and heading to the house. Have a good night, Will."

Mr. Mac continued making his rounds. Lemmie Butler and the maintenance men left the building and headed home.

That same evening, Jake McQuaid got home from work later than usual just as daylight was fading from the sky. Winona was quick to notice the smell of beer on Jake's breath when she greeted him at the door and gave him a kiss on the cheek. She was used to the usual odor of his sweaty clothes stained with dirt and grease by the time he got home from work. She always thought he smelled and looked like a real man should with his wide, red chin and thick, tanned arms that seemed so strong to her when he held her. However, Winona always told Granny that Jake was gentle as a lamb around her and the kids.

"You've been celebrating." she remarked. "I just put the twins in bed for the night."

"I just had one beer, Honey. That well came in today right before quitting time when I was working the nest. I had to get down outta there in a hurry. Everybody's fine though... even the new kid I was training. I had to send for the engineer before doing anything else. Jaffe came out and had a beer with us to celebrate. Where's my baby girl?"

"She's playing on the back porch with Vera."

Vera's family, the Hendrix's, lived only a block away, and even though Vera was a year younger than Lataine, they had become good friends and attended the same church. In fact, to show how quaint things can be, Vera would meet and marry my Uncle Gerald later in her life.

Winona could tell her husband was pleased by his success at work that day, and she was happy for him... happier yet that he was still alive and well. She knew how dangerous it was bringing in oil and gas wells, having been raised in the oilfields with her brothers and uncles who had done the same kind of work for most of their lives around Luling, Texas. She had heard the stories of men getting killed and had witnessed her brother's injuries firsthand. One of her uncles had even lost the use of one of his arms working on a drilling rig. Injuries of that sort were not uncommon.

Lataine heard her daddy come in the front door. She and Vera had been playing jacks on their screened-in back porch. Their two-bedroom, wood-framed 'shotgun' house was simple but cozy, and large enough for the family and a few guests. Friends and family members often came over to visit and play dominoes for hours on end in the evenings and on weekends.

Jake had built his home on the Pilgreen Lease during their first year in New London, while he and his family were still living in a tent. Papa Dee had helped him haul in beams for the foundation, hammer out the framing, wire the whole house for electricity, build the outhouse and even finish the roof. The McQuaids had spent many an evening playing dominoes with Papa Dee and Granny.

Although Papa Dee and Granny had to live in a tent for a while in Oklahoma when Uncle Gerald was a baby, by the time they moved to Talco in 1937, Papa Dee could afford a place to rent until he built his own house in the Humble Camp. Jake and Winona were both grateful that Papa Dee and Granny had helped them get out of that tent and into a place with a roof over their heads so they could stay warm in the winter.

Mother told us that later on, when she was six years old, Papa Dee would once again be transferred from Talco to Big Sandy, Texas where no housing was available. Of necessity, her family would have to live in a tent again. By that time the whole experience of being uprooted and transferred from place to place by Humble and having to contend with substandard living conditions was more than Papa Dee was willing to accept. After two weeks of his family living in a tent, Papa Dee drove to the main Humble headquarters in Houston and told the higher-ups there that he was going to quit if they didn't get him out of Big Sandy, in spite of having given them fourteen years of loyal service. As a compromise, he accepted a temporary assignment in Crowley, Louisiana until they could send him back to Talco.

When Jake finally got home on this evening, Lataine said goodbye to her friend Vera and ran to the front of the house yelling, "Daddy, Daddy, Daddy! You're home! You're home!" She was smiling from ear to ear as she grabbed him around the waist. Jake was thrilled and picked up the youngster in his big, grease-stained hands and hoisted her into the air above his head.

"I can touch the roof now, Daddy!" trilled Lataine, as she reached with one hand and placed it on the ceiling above her.

Jake lowered her down gently and knelt down on

one knee to look his daughter straight in the eyes. Then he asked, "Did you learn anything new in school today, Sweetheart?"

"Yes, Daddy. I learned that we don't get out early tomorrow because of the PTA meeting, and my best friend Betty is going to sing and play the piano after school in the auditorium. Can you come and listen to her, too?"

"Probably not, Baby. I'll most likely be moving my rig at that time, but maybe your momma can go and bring you home." Jake looked over at Winona, hoping she hadn't made other plans. Winona nodded as if to say she was planning to go. She had already made arrangements to ride to the school and back with Glenn's mother, Edwina, for the PTA meeting.

Lataine acted disappointed, but Jake could tell it was mostly to please him. Then she asked, "In that case, will you take us to school in the morning so I can drive the truck again?"

Jake agreed, but told her she could only drive while they were going through the lease. Lataine was only ten, but he sometimes let her sit in his lap and hold the steering wheel for the short drive through the neighborhood or when they were out on an oil lease property where there was no traffic and very little danger to worry about.

Some of the older boys in Lataine's fifth grade class had already started driving without any supervision. Two years before, in 1935, the Texas legislature had debated the issue of whether or not Texans had a "God-given unalienable RIGHT TO DRIVE". A law was passed that year granting any applicant over the age of 14 a state driver's license, without any requirements for testing. That law would change again in 1937.

"Can we take Glenn with us to school tomorrow, Daddy? I can go over to his house tonight and make sure it's OK with his mom."

"Sure, Baby... haven't y'all eaten supper yet?" Jake could smell the aroma of a fresh pot of red beans Winona had been cooking, along with fried potatoes, bacon, cornbread, spinach and deviled eggs. The odors were tantalizing, and he was hungry as a bear, having eaten nothing but a handful of peanuts since his sack lunch.

Jake started to sit down on the big chair in the living room when Winona reached out and took him by the arm before he could land on her new furniture. "You need to clean up some before you get too relaxed, Honey. Supper will be ready when you get out of the washroom."

Jake took the hint and headed for the washroom he and Papa Dee had built behind the house. As he splashed cold water on his face to rinse off the soap, he thanked God for his family. Jake looked forward to the day when he could share some of what he knew with his two sons. He then began wondering again what Lataine might become when she became a mature woman and struck out on her own. The apple of his eye, she was extremely smart and could be anything she desired.

Shaking himself out of his reverie, Jake dried off and went back into the house, carrying little more than a gnawing appetite and his hope for a quiet evening at home with his wife and children.

8. Spring Fever

Lataine could hardly wait for supper to be over so she could go tell Glenn that her father was going to let her drive his truck the following morning. As she walked the two doors down to his house, she was almost unaware of the sounds of a whippoorwill calling, crickets chirping or the roar of a drilling rig in the distance. These sounds were so familiar to her that they blended into what felt like a perfect evening.

Seeing Glenn standing outside his house, she ran up to him and exclaimed, "Daddy's going to take us both to school in the morning if you can go. He's gonna let me drive his truck through the lease. I said I would ask your mom if you want to go with us."

Lataine knew that Glenn wasn't shy, but she had often observed that he acted differently when they happened to be alone together. They had been friends since both of their families had arrived in New London and had to live in the tent-camp. A couple of years before, three older boys had Glenn surrounded and tried to get him into a fistfight he couldn't win. Lataine picked up a cane fishing pole at the time and began swinging at the older bullies. She did hit a couple of them, but no one was hurt. They started laughing so hard at the sight of the frail, eight-year-old girl swinging a twelve-foot cane pole around in the air that they lost all interest in Glenn and walked away doubled over with laughter. Even at that tender age, Glenn had been impressed by Lataine's protectiveness of him. That particular incident seemed to have put a different emphasis on his feelings for her.

Glenn told Lataine, "Momma will be calling me to come in in a few minutes. Besides, she's planning to take us home from school tomorrow after the PTA meeting, so I think it will be OK." They soon had his mother's permission for him to ride to school with them the next day, and Glenn's mom told him he could stay outside for a few more minutes. Everything seemed perfect in Lataine's world.

Before returning home, Lataine had one more request. Looking up at him beseechingly, she asked, "Glenn, will you sit with me in the auditorium after class when Betty sings and plays *Danny Boy* for everybody? I want to be in the front row so I can see and hear everything."

Glenn said, "Sure, I reckon we can do that." He paused to collect his thoughts, and then continued. "You know, they've been asking me to join the junior choir at church. Would you like to be in it too?"

Lataine was somewhat surprised by Glenn's invitation. She didn't know he had any interest in singing at all. "Sure!" she exclaimed, "That'll be fun! I want to learn to play the piano, too. Daddy said we might be able to afford one at the end of the year when his bonus money comes in for drilling all those new wells."

"OK, then… we'll tell the pastor this Sunday." Glenn was feeling proud of his accomplishment until he heard Lataine's next comment.

"Maybe when we get married one day, you can sing, and I'll play the piano!" Glenn stared at her, not knowing how to react. Lataine halfway laughed, threw her hands in the air and made a double spin that sent her dress into a whirl, like girls her age are apt to do from time to time when they are feeling happy and free as the wind.

Glenn's four-year-old brother, Tommy, opened the door and announced that it was time for Glenn to come in and study. His mother peered out of the door above the youngster's head to confirm the order. Lataine told them all goodnight. They watched her run back across the street to her house, then turn and wave back when she opened her front door. Glenn kept watching Lataine until she made it safely inside, wondering all the while what the future might truly hold for the two of them.

9. *Homework and Dreams*

Winona McQuaid was finishing up after doing the dishes when Lataine returned from across the street. Jake was bouncing his young twins on his knees to the rhythm of Roy Acuff singing a soft country song on the radio called *You're the Only Star in My Blue Heaven*. The twin boys were about a year old. They had awakened when Jake went into his bedroom to change into a clean pair of long-handled underwear for the evening. Today folks sit around watching their high definition, plasma TV's, but back then they sat around and listened to the radio.

Although war was on the horizon in Europe during this post-Depression era in 1937, most Americans were feeling positive that the economy had improved. The average family income was around $150 a month. A new car cost $760, a loaf of bread was 9 cents, and a gallon of milk was 50 cents. This was the year that saw the opening of the Golden Gate Bridge in San Francisco. The world would witness the explosion of the Hindenburg airship two months later on May 6th when NBC radio announcer Herb Morrison went to New Jersey to do a routine voice-over for a newsreel. His broadcast would become an emotional, on-the-scene description of a calamity nobody expected.

Most U.S. airships of the time were already using

helium (a by-product of natural gas) to stay airborne, but hydrogen was ten to twenty times less expensive. One third of the world's helium reserves are located in Texas. Using hydrogen for air travel was still considered safe in German zeppelins before that event occurred. Thirty-five of the Hindenburg's ninety-seven passengers and crew were killed, as well as one member of the ground crew.

Later that same year on July 2, 1937, the world would learn the fate of Amelia Earhart, as radio broadcasts throughout the world announced that her aircraft was lost somewhere over the vast Pacific Ocean during her final attempt to fly around the world.

The majority of Americans had not yet fully embraced the notion of "Whatever can go wrong, will go wrong." However, apart from an inordinate amount of luck or divine intervention, history and *Murphy's Law* tend to support the idea. It would take another world war, Hitler's Holocaust in Europe, nuclear proliferation and the advent of the cold war in the following generation to mark any turning point toward the end of America's "age of innocence".

Robert Redford was born in 1937, as were Bill Cosby and Mary Tyler Moore. FDR was still president and doing radio talks. Walt Disney was having great success with his new animated production of *Snow White and the Seven Dwarfs* ...and it was even in color!

Radio in the '30s had the impact that TV generates today. Over 80% of the population had at least one radio, and millions had radios in their cars. On January 25th *The Guiding Light* debuted on NBC Radio, sparking the popularity of daytime soap operas. Judy Garland sang on a live show every week or two on CBS Radio, and March 14th marked the beginning of a new comedy series starring Jack Benny and Fred Allen. *The Amos and Andy Show* continued to get good ratings, and NBC Radio featured Drew Barrymore's grandfather, the legendary stage actor John Barrymore, in his production of Shakespeare's *Taming of the Shrew.* There were also a number of crime dramas and popular westerns like *The Lone Ranger* being broadcast regularly on radio. But on this night, Jake and Winona were simply enjoying their favorite music.

Lataine scooted up on the arm of her daddy's big chair and leaned her head on his shoulder. She was still thinking about her visit with Glenn. She reached over to pat one of her baby brothers on the belly and laughed as she removed the other one's pacifier. Then, just as quickly, she put it back in his mouth causing him to giggle. Jake asked his daughter, "Sugar, do you have any homework you need to do tonight? It's gettin' kinda late."

Lataine remembered her last class assignment and ran to collect her geography book and a piece of paper. Then she took a seat at the kitchen table and began to trace the outline of a map of Texas.

"What are the most abundant natural resources in the region of Texas where we live?" Lataine read the first question at the end of Chapter 12 aloud, hoping for a quick answer from her mom or dad.

Jake answered, "We've mainly got a lot of oil and natural gas under the ground here. If not for that, your nice new school wouldn't have been built, and you would be doing your lessons somewhere else besides here in New London."

Winona turned her head and gave Jake one of those looks that told him to be a bit more serious. Then she explained to Lataine, "Your Daddy's right, Sweetheart. Oil and gas are indeed our greatest mineral blessing in this area, but there is also cotton, lumber, water, farmland and cattle."

Lataine made a note on her paper under the map that she had now divided into separate regions and decided that she liked math better than geography and English class better than either of those. She began looking through her book to find the answers that would complete her assignment, while the twin boys fell asleep on their daddy's lap in front of the radio.

Jake told his wife, "I wish Clemmie and Dee were here right now. We could play a game of dominoes. I don't think I ever had more fun than watching Dee when he gets mad at Clemmie for playing against his hand." A big grin spread over his face. "I bet there are already a few dents in the walls of their new house in Talco from him slamming his dominoes off the table!"

Winona responded by saying, "I sometimes feel bad for Clemmie when he does that. She doesn't seem to mind though and just laughs it off."

"I've never seen a man get so worked up over a game." mused Jake. "One time we were playing three-handed Moon, and Clemmie got way behind. Instead of getting upset about it, she said a little prayer out loud for Jesus to help her out. On the next bid, she shot the moon and won the game. Dee was holding his last domino and slammed it down on the table so hard it split in half. Dee said he was not going to play with her if she had to pray to win. I thought I was going to die laughing! Of course that was the last game we could play until we got ourselves a new set of dominoes."

Winona folded her dishtowel, laid it on the countertop and said, "It's too late to start anything new tonight, Honey. I've got a big day tomorrow with the PTA meeting and all. The boys are apt to wear me out when I have to take care of them away from the house." Winona picked up one of the twins and motioned for Jake to follow her with the other one to put them back in their bed. When she returned to the kitchen, Winona asked Lataine if she needed anymore help with her homework.

Lataine had just laid her head on her book and looked up at her mother with sleepy eyes. Winona could see the young girl was done for the evening. She carefully escorted Lataine to bed and decided to call it a night. Winona McQuaid would later recall how blessed she felt that night having her husband by her side and all of their beautiful children safely tucked in for a good night's rest. If there were any crickets chirping in their house that night, no one seemed to mind.

On that same night, Billy and Ollie were snuggled safely in their beds, but they were having nightmares about deadly snakes. They knew that long after this lucky Saint Patrick's Day was over, those poisonous vipers would still be slithering just below the surface of the water where the boys had been splashing and swimming without a care in the world. Billy would wake up the next morning wishing he lived in Ireland.

Thursday
March 18, 1937

10. A Spring Morning

The next morning dawned bright and clear in New London, Texas. It was ten days before Easter Sunday and eight days before Good Friday, the day that Passover began that year.

As most folks know, Good Friday is set aside each year to remember the Passover when Jesus died on the cross for the sins of the world. The original Passover is remembered as the night in which the Lord protected all of the Israelites who did what Moses told them. They sacrificed a lamb and spattered its blood on their doorposts. Then they roasted it for supper and ate the entire animal, along with bitter herbs and unleavened bread, while standing shod and fully clothed with a staff in their hands. On that particular night, an act of God killed all the remaining firstborn of Egypt, both man and beast. "Pharaoh and all his officials and all the Egyptians got up during the night, and there was loud wailing in Egypt, for there was not a house without someone dead." (Exodus 12:30)

After that happened, the surviving Israelites would wander in a harsh desert for 40 years before reclaiming their promised land. Based on what I have learned since first reading that story as a child, it probably took about the same amount of time for most of the families in Egypt to fully recover from the loss of their children that night.

I feel quite certain that God made this fifth day of the week. (After all, who else could we give credit for that?) However, most calamities that occur on such days usually result from individuals making bad decisions. It was Pharaoh's refusal to do what Moses demanded that led to the biblical disasters that plagued Egypt. Hindsight is indeed 20/20. Perhaps the Lord simply passed through the small town of New London on this fine spring morning, thinking everything was just fine and dandy. That's what Jake McQuaid did after dropping off his daughter and the neighbor's boy at school.

When Jake parked his vehicle to leave the kids at school, Lataine kissed her daddy on the cheek and thanked him for letting her sit on his lap and hold the steering wheel. Then he went on to work, looking forward to the evening when he would again be with the family he loved so dearly.

When he arrived at his drilling site, Jake learned that the hole pressure on the well they brought in the evening before had dropped off. The engineers were convinced they had just hit a small gas pocket and that the main oil and gas reservoir was still waiting to be tapped somewhere below it. With that news, Jake scratched his head and thought to himself, *I can't recall ever seeing a gas pressure build up that dropped off to nothing overnight. Where could that pressurized gas have gone?* Regardless, there was nothing left to do but to keep drilling the hole deeper. Jake's men were on salary anyway, so without hesitation or any further discussion on the matter they just picked up where they had left off the day before.

After having exited her father's truck at the school, Lataine took Glenn by the hand and asked him to help her look for her friend Betty. They soon spotted her beside one of the buildings with another friend of theirs named Ruby. The three girls were very close and often went to see movies together on Saturday afternoons.

"Where on earth have you been, girl?" asked Lataine. "Are you still singing after class today? I wish I was. Glenn and me are gonna sit up in the front row to watch you perform. You'll get out of class early since you're in the music program tomorrow in Henderson. Me and Glenn are gonna start singing in the junior choir at church. Were you sick yesterday? I missed you in class... Do you want to join us Ruby?"

When Betty finally got a chance to speak, she said, "I just wasn't feeling quite right yesterday, so Mama told me I could stay home and rest my voice. I'm so happy y'all want to hear me sing. I've been practicing *Danny Boy* for over two weeks now. I never knew you were interested in singing. I thought you just wanted to play the piano?"

"I do! But I have to wait until the end of the year

when Daddy gets enough money to buy one from all the oil wells he's drilling. I decided last night that I want to learn to sing too."

The first bell rang letting everyone know classes would begin in fifteen minutes. Betty begged Lataine and Ruby to go to the office with her to drop off the note signed by her mother excusing her for being out of school the day before. "It will just take a minute. If I'm late for class, I don't want to walk in the room by myself. Will y'all …Ple-e-e-ase ???"

Ruby declined Betty's request, saying that she had to go all the way to the other end of the school from the office to get to her next class.

With a mischievous grin on her face, Lataine asked, "Betty, would it be OK if I tell the principal you slept in the barn and woke up a little hoarse?" Betty wasn't amused and rolled her eyes, as Ruby turned away from them and headed for her first class. Lataine continued, "OK, I won't tell him that, but you will owe me a favor when I need one someday."

When Lataine and Betty entered the principal's office, they saw Mr. Waggoner's secretary, Marie Patterson. Most of the students called her Miss Mary. She looked up from her desk and greeted them, "Good morning girls, can I help you with something?"

Lataine was the first to speak up. "Betty was sick

yesterday, so she brought a note from home. I came in to talk for her, since she needs to save her voice for singing and playing the piano at the Henderson meet tomorrow."

"That is so sweet of you, Lataine." Miss Mary could hardly hide the grin that was about to betray her amusement at Lataine's story when Betty handed her the note signed by her mom. "I'll pass this along to Mr. Waggoner the next time he comes out of his office. Are you feeling better today, Dear?"

Betty began to respond, but could only manage a "Yes, Ma'am..." before Lataine interrupted her.

"That sure is a pretty ring on your finger, Miss Mary. Did you get one for Christmas like I did?" Lataine reached out her hand to show the secretary her gold ring, holding it within inches of Miss Mary's face. "My cousin gave me this one. Do you like it?"

Miss Mary decided to play along and said, "I really do like it, especially the little rose on top. Mine is an engagement ring. I'm getting married in June after the end of school this year." She looked down at her engagement ring and smiled, tilting her head slightly to the left. Then she looked back up at the two girls who both let out an almost indiscernible sigh. "Now... both of you better hightail it to your first class, or you'll be back in here soon with a pink tardy slip and have to talk with Mr. Waggoner in person."

"Yes, Ma'am." Lataine replied. "Glenn and me are getting married too someday. He's gonna sing and I'm gonna play the piano when we get married."

Betty's eyes opened wide when she heard her friend's revelation, but she didn't say a word. Instead, she reached out and pulled Lataine by the elbow to lead her out of the office. Lataine waved goodbye to Marie Patterson as they headed for the door. Miss Mary offered a final remark to Betty, "I hope you sing well tomorrow, Sweetie. I'll be listening in the audience. Bye for now." Marie shook her head and smiled to herself when the girls left the room. They reminded her of her own schooldays just a few years before.

When they were halfway down the hall toward their first class, Lataine got an earful from her friend. "What's all this stuff about you and Glenn getting married? I guess you were gonna tell everybody in the whole world before you told your best friend, huh?" The second school bell of the day rang just as Lataine and Betty entered the door to their first class. Betty gave Lataine a royal stare to emphasize that she was still angry with her, but Lataine just rolled her eyes and took her seat. Both girls looked up attentively toward the front of the room as their teacher warned the students about the need for everyone to be in their seats before the bell rang. There were other students who hadn't yet made it to school at all that day.

11. Playing Hooky

Kenneth was another of Lataine's classmates. He and his younger sister Elsie lived a few miles out of town in a house off the main road. The children were picked up and dropped off by the school bus every day at the same spot beside the road, which could not be seen from their house because of brush and trees. Normally, they would listen for the bus to pass by in the morning before going outside. The bus driver would honk the horn when he initially drove past their house to make sure Kenneth and Elsie were waiting beside the road when he returned for them. The bus would then travel about a mile further, pick up the neighbor's children, turn around, and stop again to pick up Kenneth and Elsie on the return trip heading back to the school. The children only had a few minutes after they heard the bus pass by and honk until it returned to pick them up.

A few weeks earlier, an uncle of Kenneth and Elsie had given them a small, curly-haired cocker spaniel puppy, which they named Rusty. They were both extremely fond of it. Rusty followed the children everywhere and typically followed them when they walked to the road and got on the bus.

On the morning of March 18th, the children were ready for school early and were outside playing with Rusty near the main road when the bus first arrived. When the bus driver saw them, he stopped and picked them up. He then proceeded down the road to the neighbor's house and turned around for the trip back. Instead of going back to the house, Rusty remained beside the road where Kenneth and Elsie had gotten on the bus. When the bus passed by on its return trip to school, the puppy ran beneath its wheels. The children looked out of the rear windows to see the body of their beloved canine companion lying in the middle of the road. Kenneth's heart sank, and Elsie was visibly shaken. Both ran to the front of the bus and asked the driver to stop and let them off, which he did. They immediately rushed back to see their dying puppy.

"Is Rusty dead, Kenny?" asked the younger Elsie.

"I'm afraid so, Sis." Kenneth picked up the little dog. It was still warm, but no longer moving. He told Elsie, "I don't want to go to school today. We need to bury Rusty and not tell Pa, or he'll make us go to school. He's liable to be awful mad, seein' as how Uncle Butch gave him to us, and we went and let him get run over by the bus."

"Not tell Pa? And skip school? What about tellin' Momma?" Elsie was already upset, but certainly didn't want to get into trouble.

"We best keep this to ourselves and stay hid behind the barn today. I know where there's a shovel in the shed to bury Rusty with, and I can't leave you by yourself to make it to school on your own." Kenneth was convinced that his plan for both he and his sister was the only solution to their dilemma.

Elsie was soon persuaded by her older brother's insistence that she stay with him, rather than walking back to their house. Both children followed a narrow trail through the woods that led them to the barn behind their house. They were careful to stay out of sight, while keeping an eye out for snakes. Kenneth located his daddy's shovel from the tool shed and had soon dug a hole in the soft earth behind their barn.

When the time came to place the dead puppy in its shallow grave, Elsie asked her older brother, "Kenny, do you think we should say a prayer for Rusty? He was such a good puppy." She covered her face with both hands to try and hide her tears from her brother.

"I reckon we should... let me think." Kenneth decided he ought to say some kind of prayer to help make Elsie feel better. He removed his skullcap that was identical his friend Billy's, placed it over his chest, and began to speak while looking skyward, "God... Rusty here was a good puppy and didn't ever do anything wrong that we know about. He just hadn't ever learned not to chase the bus and went and got his self killed. And if you decide to keep him, I'd bet he'd make a real good hunting dog for ya' when he grows up." He paused, trying to decide if anything more needed to be said. "Can you think of anything else you want to say, Sis?"

Elsie was still somewhat overwhelmed, but seemed satisfied with Kenneth's prayer. "I just wish Rusty was still OK, and we were at school right now."

"I'm sorry, Sis. You'll feel better tomorrow. We both will." said Kenneth.

"I know, Kenny." said Elsie. "It's just that I like school, and we're missin' it now. I miss Rusty too."

Elsie slowly began to accept the idea that everything would be all right again soon and decided to talk about something else. "I heard that girl in your class named Lataine is a real live princess."

Kenneth was curious. "Who told you she was a princess?"

"My friend Vera who lives out on the Pilgreen lease with her." said Elsie. "She must be, 'cause she's got a real gold ring with a rose on it like they all wear."

Kenneth dismissed his little sister's fantasy. "Do you like school better than playin' hooky?" he asked. Elsie shrugged her shoulders and looked down at what was once their happy little puppy, exuberant with energy and vitality just a short time earlier that day.

He proceeded to place the puppy in the hole he had dug and shoveled the moist dirt onto its stiffening body. Afterward, he spread the dirt around the grave so that it almost appeared as if no one had disturbed the soil. Then Kenneth turned to look for his sister, who was now sitting on a bale of hay inside the edge of the barn, wondering what they would do for the rest of the day.

Kenneth went back to the tool shed and struggled with its old rickety wooden door a second time. When it finally opened, he was starting to feel angry about everything that had been happening that day. He tossed the shovel into the shed and it banged against the other tools. Then he tried to slam the door that kept dragging and getting stuck in the dirt and rocks.

By that time, their mother was hanging the clothes from her morning wash in their back yard and heard the noises coming from the tool shed. Rather than investigate herself, she dropped her laundry basket, ran inside the house, and asked her husband to go check it out. He pocketed a handful of shells and went outside carrying his double-barreled shotgun.

When he came around the side of his barn, he immediately saw Elsie sitting on the bale of hay and Kenneth meandering slowly back to the barn from the tool shed. Both children froze motionless as their father stared back and forth at them in bewilderment, still grasping his loaded shotgun. In spite of their pleadings and explanations, their father spanked them both and returned them to school before lunchtime. He marched them both to the principal's office, and made them apologize to Mr. Waggoner for their absences. The children had to convince both men that it would never happen again. Elsie and Kenneth were told to stay at the school until their mother picked them up when she came back in the afternoon for the PTA meeting.

While both children waited in the quiet hallway for their father to finish talking with Mr. Waggoner, Kenneth whispered to his little sister, "I told you Pa would be mad if he found out we let Rusty get killed."

Both children were momentarily startled when the noon bell in the hallway above their heads rang unexpectedly, announcing the time for lunch recess. They pressed themselves against the wall as excited students scampered out of their classrooms and scattered in every direction. Some headed straight for the main exits to go outside and enjoy the fresh air while others headed in the opposite direction toward the cafeteria.

12. King of the Mountain

Outside during their lunch recess, Betty was still trying to get to the bottom of what Lataine had told the school secretary, Miss Mary, about her and Glenn getting married.

"Lataine, did Glenn ask you to marry him? What happened? You have to tell me all the details." Betty demanded.

Lataine explained to her friend, "Well, Betty. I went over to Glenn's house last night to see if he wanted to ride with me to school this morning, and he asked me if I wanted to join the choir with him at church. There can only be one reason why he would ask me that, so I told him I would. Anyway, we're going to talk to the pastor about joining the choir this Sunday when we go to church together. I told Glenn I was also going to learn to play the piano, and that one day when we get married I would play the piano, and he could sing. After that, we couldn't talk anymore because his little brother and his momma came to the front door and told him to come inside and do his homework. It's not like we're sending out invitations tomorrow! I haven't said anything to anyone except you and Miss Mary... and you better not either!"

Betty rolled her eyes and said, "I might tell Ruby." Then she continued, "I suppose now you're expecting me to dance at your wedding with a cowbell on for going with me to the office this morning, huh?"

"That would be funny, Betty. Would ya'? Would ya' ...Ple-e-e-ase ???" mocked Lataine, with a mischievous grin on her face. Betty slapped Lataine on her shoulder with her empty lunch sack, and both girls had a good laugh. Their friend, Ruby, arrived to join the girls and wanted to know what they were laughing about.

Betty decided not to divulge what Lataine had confided to her until later that day and told Ruby, "Oh, we were just talking about Glenn Belcher."

Lataine said to Ruby, "He's kind of handsome, don't you think?"

Not waiting for any reply, Lataine looked over toward Glenn and Joe Bo, who were standing a few yards away watching some older boys who were playing "King of the Mountain" on the main gas pipe that was exposed at the entrance to the auditorium. One of the bigger boys was jumping up and down on the two-inch pipe near the brick wall where it went into the basement's dead air space. There, smaller pipes connected that led to the 72 gas heaters located in every room throughout the building. The school janitor had made those connections, but had made no provision for regulating the gas flow.

Lataine was momentarily distracted by the sound of a crack or thud, as if a sixteen-pound monkey wrench had just dropped into a hole some distance away. She glanced over at the boys Glenn and Joe Bo had been watching with envy. Glenn looked over at Lataine and momentarily caught her eyes, as if to confirm that he had also heard that same noise coming from beneath the gas pipe. She knew those boys were not supposed to be playing on the pipe, but just as Lataine looked back in their direction, the boys caught sight of the principal, Mr. Waggoner, returning from lunch and walking up the nearby sidewalk to enter the building. They took off running in the other direction.

At the time, no one even considered the possibility that damage may have been caused by the boys' playful infraction. There were no obvious signs of it. The school bell rang announcing the beginning of afternoon classes, and all the children who were outside re-entered the building.

It was a warm afternoon, so there was no need for additional heat in any of the classrooms, and no one would notice any significant drop in the hot water temperature at the bathroom sinks. The school day continued to move along in seemingly typical fashion, but there would soon be nothing typical about it at all.

13. The Crawlspace

After lunch when afternoon classes began, Lemmie Butler started moving his freshly painted stage props to the gym with the help of his afternoon students and the two maintenance men from the evening before. Lemmie's Industrial Arts students had painted murals on the newly built stage props earlier that morning. The dance instructor in charge of that afternoon's PTA presentation was very pleased. She asked Lemmie and his helpers to set them up and arrange them in the gym while she supervised. The entire process took up the remainder of the first class of the afternoon.

After they had set up all of the freshly painted murals, the music director stopped into the gym to see the new set decorations. She was so impressed by his work that she asked Lemmie if he could make a similar one with a few minor design changes to sit on the auditorium stage. She needed a standing wooden frame where she could post a large announcement banner for her upcoming student musical performance that was scheduled a few weeks later. She knew that many of the parents who attended the PTA meeting would come to the auditorium afterward and take note of the announcement. Lataine and Glenn were planning to meet their moms there and listen to Betty and the other music students perform before heading home for

An Empty Tomb (CS)

the day. Other parents had made similar plans to meet their children in the auditorium after the PTA meeting.

Lemmie thought he could do what the music director wanted during his next woodshop class by re-designing a used prop from the year before and agreed to her proposal. The first thing that had to be done was to remove one of the used stage props from the crawlspace in the basement next to the woodshop where they were being stored.

Lemmie asked the maintenance men to unlock the crawlspace door so his students could retrieve a reusable prop to work with. He assigned Billy, Ollie and Kenneth to the task and gave them specific instructions for what he wanted them to locate and return to the woodworking area.

The storage area in the crawlspace was unlit. They could only see inside by the light entering through the door from the shop. Before they entered, the senior maintenance man told the boys, "It can get really hot in that storage area boys, so y'all be real careful moving stuff around. And don't take too long or you'll get overheated."

The head janitor was always concerned about the safety of the students and took every precaution when working around dangerous equipment or tools. Nevertheless, he was a *Jack of all trades, but a master of none.* He pulled his large key ring from his belt and unlocked the crawlspace door. The boys entered one at a time.

All seemed a bit too quiet inside the crawlspace. Any noises emanating from the rest of the school were dampened by its thick concrete walls, and the only noises heard inside became amplified echoes made by the intruders themselves. It was like an empty tomb.

The head maintenance man waited outside the open door for a couple of minutes while biting off a fresh chaw of tobacco. He decided to call his helper over and sent him inside to assist the boys. All of a sudden, he heard a crash. Plywood inside the storage area began to fall like oversized dominoes. He looked inside to find his helper and the three boys laughing and reaching down to pick up a pile of broken sticks and old plywood props.

"I think we found a good one to use!" yelled Billy, while making an obvious effort to suppress his laughter over the broken stage decorations that had somehow fallen and surprised everyone.

The senior maintenance worker was not amused. He continued staring through the doorway into the crawlspace, while shaking his head at the scattered mess on the floor and the plywood that had fallen. Pieces of wood were now leaning against the network of natural gas pipes that funneled fuel in every direction toward the 72 gas heaters in the building. If there was any damage to the pipes, no one took notice or reported it.

It took another fifteen minutes or so for the students and the maintenance workers to re-stack the plywood sheets, discard the broken pieces, exit the crawlspace and take the best piece to the woodworking area. The boys were sweating and breathing heavily before they finished their assigned task.

Ollie told Lemmie he wasn't feeling well. His face appeared redder than usual. He was told to drink some water, have a seat and cool off or report to the nurse. Billy was also feeling light-headed and decided to sit down, thinking he had just gotten too hot working in that dead air space. Kenneth's eyes were tearing up, and he felt sick to his stomach. He was still thinking about his dog Rusty and still feeling sad.

Students had been reporting headaches and watery eyes for the past few weeks, and there were similar complaints on this day. Such complaints were readily chalked up to allergies or late-winter colds. It was, after all, almost spring in East Texas, and the air was filled with pollens.

The younger maintenance man complained to his partner of a headache, so they decided it was time for a short break. One of them went across the street in front of the school to get a coke, but no one thought to shut and lock the door to the crawlspace.

14. *From Blessing to Bane*

As the last class of the day began, Billy, Ollie and Kenneth were feeling better. They had left the basement workshop and were again seated in Miss Wright's class. Lemmie's last group of shop students were helping him complete the work on his final project of the day.

A mini-exodus from the school was taking place. Grades one through four were lining up outside for the buses to take them home. Young Vera, Lataine's playmate from down the street, promptly left the gymnasium to catch her regular bus after having participated in one of the first dance performances that were held for the parents that came early for the PTA meeting.

Four piano students, including Betty, were practicing in the auditorium for the Henderson meet scheduled on the following day.

Kenneth's sister, Elsie, and many other elementary school children, had been instructed by their parents to wait for them until they arrived for the PTA meeting. They were absent from the bus lines and most were spending their free time playing outside or waiting for their moms and dads in the gym.

Vera climbed aboard her bus. As it began to leave the school, she looked through the rear window and tried to catch a glimpse of her friend, Elsie, who had been upset most of the afternoon. Vera usually shared a seat with her on the bus, but Elsie was with her mother in the gym when the bus left the school.

Mrs. Wright's class had a number of vacant desks since her students who were in the dance program had gone to the gym, and those participating in the Henderson meet had gone to the auditorium. She told her remaining students that after they went over the lesson plan for the day, there would be some time left to study or visit quietly, but that they must remain in the room for the entire class period.

Billy raised his hand and asked, "Why don't we get to leave too? They're no better than the rest of us… even if we're not in the Henderson meet or in a dance class." Some of the others snickered at Billy's remarks.

Mrs. Wright responded by telling Billy, "I'm sure you all have someplace you would rather be during this period, but I was told to keep everyone here until the end of class. So, let's make good use of the time we have today."

Mrs. Wright instructed her students to take out their homework assignments from the night before and turn to the questions at the end of Chapter 12. She asked Mary to read the first question aloud to the class.

Mary began reading, "What are the most abundant natural resources in the region of Texas where you live?" Lataine raised her hand before Mary finished reading.

"Would you like to answer the first question, Lataine?" asked Mrs. Wright, as she moved to the blackboard and picked up a piece of chalk with which to write.

"Yes, Ma'am." Lataine looked down at her homework and started to read. "Oil and natural gas are East Texas' greatest mineral blessings. Without them this school would not be here and none of us would be here learning our lessons!" Mrs. Wright wrote her words on the chalkboard as Lataine read.

The teacher then asked the class, "Does anyone else have a different answer?" None of the students responded. Mrs. Wright continued. "Lataine, do you have anything more to add?"

"No Ma'am. It was getting late last night, and I fell asleep at the kitchen table after writing that down." The other students laughed out loud. Even Ollie couldn't keep from holding back a laugh, but he quickly covered his face and looked back down at his book.

Mrs. Wright prompted the students to pay attention to the lesson and asked if anyone had a written response to Question #2.

Billy raised his hand again, and told Mrs. Wright, "I've got my map you told us to draw, but you only said to be prepared to answer the chapter questions… not to write 'em down."

"In that case, I hope most of you are better prepared when we meet for class on Monday. The rest of the students will be here then, and we will discuss the remaining questions together. How does that sound to everyone?" The students nodded and expressed their agreement with Mrs. Wright's suggestion.

All of the students were anxiously anticipating a long weekend away from school since Friday classes had been cancelled. The teacher asked them to turn in their maps and get together in small groups. Lataine turned around and smiled at Glenn, who moved to the vacant desk next to hers. There was some shuffling about as the students did as instructed and moved to sit with their most familiar classmates. Then Mrs. Wright assigned each group one of the remaining questions and instructed them to prepare a written answer for Monday's class. She knew the students would be able to visit among themselves this way and learn something useful as well.

Mrs. Wright assigned Kenneth to act as classroom monitor so she could go to the PTA meeting in the gym and reminded the students once again to remain seated until the final bell rang.

In the basement woodworking shop, Lemmie Butler looked up at the clock on the wall and realized the time was approaching three o'clock in the afternoon. Betty was on stage with her peers in the auditorium, rehearsing her upcoming performance of *Danny Boy*. A few students were walking to the gym to join their teachers and parents at the PTA meeting. The junior and senior high students were getting ready to cast their ballots in the school elections.

Lemmie Butler decided it was time to get his final project completed and ready to move to the auditorium. He told two of his last period students, John Dow and Judson Woolley, to finish up what they were working on and help him move it.

They put away their tools, and then bent down to pick up the wooden stage prop. Judson suddenly got an unexpected splinter in his hand from the rough edge of the plywood.

For safety's sake, Lemmie decided it would be worth the extra time and effort to smooth down the edges of the wood before trying to move it again. He instructed the boys to put on their gloves and set the plywood on an empty table so it could be sanded. He reached for a hand sander and began to work on the rough wooden edges, being careful not to hit any bare nail heads that always made sparks fly. Sawdust had been accumulating on the floor throughout the day.

Another student, Bud Watson, was doing some welding in the front of the room. Lemmie believed it was a perfect time to teach Judson how to use the sander and told him to go easy on the nail heads in the wood.

Judson began using the hand sander and accidentally pushed in the button on the side of the handle that kept the switch depressed and the machine running. He lifted it away from the wood as it continued to run wildly and looked over at his shop teacher inquiringly, while moving his forefinger back and forth to show him he was no longer depressing the switch. Lemmie understood what had happened and reached to unplug the cord of the hand sander Judson was holding. He checked the clock again, and it read 3:15 pm. He decided to move the rough plywood to the industrial table sander so they could finish the job more quickly.

It was only minutes before classes were to be dismissed. Elementary school children were playing tag on the lawn between the buildings. From inside the auditorium, mothers were staring out through a large plate glass window, watching their children.

Natural gas, which is lighter than air and rises, had now penetrated throughout every available space beneath the building. The woodworking shop was filled with around thirty students. John Dow watched his shop teacher walk over to the wall socket which was approximately two feet from the partially open door going to the building's crawlspace. Another student in the basement woodworking shop switched off a band saw just as Mr. Butler reached to plug in the portable connection to the industrial sander. When the two prongs of the plug touched the wall socket, the electrical arc emitted a familiar blue flame that ignited the explosive gas in the building's crawlspace. It was 3:17 pm.

Suddenly, there was a brilliantly expanding flash of light and heat. The walls of the school bulged outward and the building exploded like an atomic bomb! It was a violent conflagration. Bricks, wooden beams and steel-reinforced concrete walls blasted in every direction. A huge section of the roof flew upward like a cork popping out of a champagne bottle. When it crashed back down, the main wing of the structure collapsed. The force of the explosion was so great that a two-ton concrete slab was thrown clear of the building. It crashed down on a 1936 Chevrolet parked 200 feet from the school where a baby lay sleeping. The vehicle was crushed like an eggshell. Falling stones wrecked another fifty cars. Some of the flying wreckage included children who were thrown through the air like torn rag dolls. Trees split in half and were blown over. A fiery ball escaped toward the clouds, singeing the atmosphere. A deafening boom penetrated every ear for miles in every direction. The explosion was so sudden and violent that it sounded as if a divine trumpet blast had been blown to summon all the angels of God from the very heights of heaven to come forth and witness the hundreds of children that were perishing at that very moment.

All four of the students who had been practicing the piano in the auditorium, including Lataine's best friend Betty, were immediately killed by the blast. In one study hall, every one of the 65 students in the room perished. Eighteen-year-old Martha Harris was in the home economics building, 180 feet away from the main building. She heard a terrible roar and felt the earth shake. Then bricks and glass came showering down. She looked out a window and saw her friends dying like flies.

The explosion was heard for miles, serving as its own alarm. It was even heard as far away as the roughneck tent-camps of Kilgore and Tyler, 35 miles to the northwest. The blast wave caused the oil derrick where Jake McQuaid was working to sway back and forth. Jake, Buster and the rest of the men at the rig looked toward the school. They immediately loaded their equipment into their vehicles and headed toward it. A giant white cloud soon began to settle over the remains of the school.

Stunned witnesses were frozen motionless, unable to process what had just happened. The bodies of innocent children were lying all over the grounds. The faces of those who were not killed outright by the blast reflected only horror. No one left alive had ever experienced such unnatural ferocity.

Vera was five miles from the school when the explosion happened. Her bus driver, Lonnie Barber, was driving up a hill on the outskirts of town when he heard a boom. Seconds later he felt a sudden gust of wind hit the vehicle. There was also a teacher at the rear of the bus who always made sure riders were aboard, seated safely and well-behaved. Mr. Barber looked back toward the school, as did all of the elementary school children. To their horror, they saw a huge cloud of smoke and debris where the school had been. Lonnie knew that most of the students and staff were still in the building. He had four children of his own that were still at the school and began rushing to take his passengers home.

Five and a half miles away, the night watchman, Mr. Mac, was plowing a field with his mule when he saw a mushroom shaped cloud rising in the air. It was followed by a blast wave that toppled trees on his farm. Everyone at his house could see the school explode into the air from that far away and even farther. Mr. Mac's four-year-old granddaughter, Ann, was climbing a tree behind his house when the blast wave hit. The tree she was in shook so hard she fell to the ground, gashing open her arm and leaving her with a scar she would carry for the rest of her life. Ann's mother, Florine, was also at the house. Florine swore that she saw body parts (arms, legs, torsos, etc.) flying into the air away from the explosion.

There were students in nearly all of the building's classrooms who were killed instantly. Catherine Hughes had been in her typing class when her math teacher, Mr. Bunch, came in and asked her to go with him to the PTA program. They left for the program early and went out the back door across the alley between the school and the gym. Just as soon as they sat down in the gym, the explosion took place. She had just left her typing class where everyone else was killed.

Preston Crim jumped from a second story window and ran, after seeing his girlfriend decapitated by a falling concrete slab. His teacher had told everyone to get under a desk when the rumbling started. His girlfriend was in plain sight of him when it happened.

Parents, children and teachers began rushing out of the gym dazed, not knowing what to do or where to go. Lataine's teacher, Mrs. Wright, and her mother, Winona, had been watching the dance performances with about fifty more mothers. Some, like Winona, had their young children with them.

Third-grader, Ollie Bullock, had just finished performing her minuet and had walked into the stands to sit down next to her mother, when the blast started rocking the wooden gymnasium back and forth. Her mother grabbed her, and they rushed outside through one of the few exit doors of the gym.

By the time Ollie and her mother finally realized what had happened, they were standing outside near the stunned principal, Mr. Waggoner, who had been heading back toward his office where two students were studying. Those students were both killed when the blast occurred, as was the school secretary, Miss Marie Patterson.

Music teacher Mattie Queen Price would soon be found by her brother, Bud Price, inside of her damaged car in the parking lot. She had been crushed by a large slab of concrete. Mattie had made prior plans to leave the school early that day to inform her brother of something important. He never learned what she planned to tell him.

The lives of those who lost children and loved ones to the London School explosion would never be the same. The shock and devastation of so many lives destroyed in a flash continued to take its toll, as survivors bore witness to the cruel fate that had spared them.

15. "Oh, my God! It's our children!"

The huge gymnasium continued to rock back and forth, as mothers and teachers were rushing to get outside. Most started coughing and choking from flying dust and ash.

Mr. Waggoner put his hands over his face and screamed, **"Oh, my God! It's our children!"** Some people began yelling, **"The world is coming to an end!"** Some thought Adolf Hitler was bombing America. Others wondered if this had been an attack by Mexico. As soon as the debris settled there was a deathly silence, almost like being in a vacuum. Everyone witnessing the scene was in shock. Soon the sounds, the screaming, the moaning, and people running all over shook most back to awareness. Bystanders began attempting whatever rescue was possible.

Only one damaged section of the main building remained standing. Injured children were staggering, tripping and falling as they tried to maneuver to safety. Some were escaping through broken windows. Others were jumping from second story walls. Dead and injured children were lying in rubble piles. A few were standing still, frozen with fear. Victims were walking about aimlessly… deafened and bewildered. A few were running away from the school toward the safety of their homes. Parents began rushing about seeking their children. Most were found dead or bleeding and critically injured.

A cloud of ash continued to drift about in the air above the surface like an enormous, dirty snowstorm. The activity was surreal, chaotic. Desperate parents became hysterical. Many were standing around the devastation in shock, unable to contain their misery and grief. Some parents began digging desperately through piles of rubble with their bare hands, listening for small voices and cries for help. Most of the bodies strewn about the grounds were either burned beyond recognition or blown to bits and pieces. Some children who were trapped beneath the rubble were choking to death, their mouths and nostrils clogged by dirt and ashes.

Winona McQuaid exited the gymnasium in disbelief, holding her twins in her arms. She stood in the same spot for what seemed to her like an eternity, looking around in horror and hearing the lamentations of others. She kept hoping at any minute to see the face of her daughter, but there was no sign of her.

Those outside had been pummeled by bricks and flying debris. Winona recognized the blood-soaked dress worn by Glenn's mother, Edwina Belcher, who had brought her to the school for the PTA meeting. Edwina had gone outside to find her son Tommy, just before the school exploded. She was lying face down about twenty yards away from her four-year-old, who was huddled and crouched against a tree trunk that had been uprooted during the blast. Nearby was Tommy's four-year-old playmate, Jimmy Phillips, who had been killed in the blast, along with Jimmy's eleven-year-old sister and fifteen-year-old brother.

Winona was unsure it really was little Tommy Belcher, because the child's face was completely covered with chalky white and gray ash mixed with blood. She walked closer and spoke Tommy's name. She only became certain that it was him when he eventually peered up at her and she looked into his eyes. An emergency worker approached them and began assisting the youngster. One of Tommy's arms appeared to have been broken and his face was bleeding. Another worker arrived immediately with a stretcher. One worker questioned Winona about the boy, noting his name and address, while the other splinted his arm and cleaned the cut on his face. They told Winona they would be transporting him to a hospital and carried little Tommy away on the stretcher.

Winona continued to walk slowly up the slope that led to the front of the school. She was careful not to trip on any of the bricks, roofing tiles, glass, concrete or metal that was scattered everywhere and blocked every path. At one point, she looked up and saw a human leg hanging from a nearby tree. She immediately looked away, trying to suppress the thought that it may have belonged to her daughter. Winona could not bear the thought of setting her babies down anywhere on this unhallowed ground. Sitting down never entered her mind, as she struggled to maintain the hope of seeing her daughter alive and well.

Jake and his crew arrived at what was left of the school within fifteen minutes after the blast. Some of his rig workers also had children at the school. Buster followed Jake, but the rest of the men were soon separated, each one doing whatever they could to locate and assist injured children. Jake began frantically walking about wild-eyed, looking for his family among the living. He soon recognized Winona carrying her precious cargo. He could tell she was in shock, as he ran to her and gently relieved her by taking the boys from her arms.

"Winona… Honey… Are you all right?" asked Jake.

For the first time since she had heard the deafening boom of the explosion, followed by the cannon blast of concrete and steel reinforcement hitting the front of the gym and landing on its roof, Winona truly began feeling what her eyes and ears had been taking in. "Jake? …Jake? Is that really you?" She reached up and placed her hands on each of his elbows that were now holding their twin boys.

"Yes, Dear… I'm here now." Jake could see no sign of outward injury to Winona and tried to assure her that she would be OK.

Winona continued to speak in a listless, subdued

tone. "I can't find her, Jake."

Jake turned to look again at the piles of twisted steel, concrete and rubble that were four or five men high in areas where the main building had once stood. No longer able to contain his fear, Jake's face contorted and his eyes began to well up with tears. He yelled out toward the overwhelming sight and heard the echo of his own voice repeating, **"Baby girl? Where are you? Lataine? ...Lataine???"**

Buster was still following Jake and reached out, offering to hold one of the twins. Jake looked at him, hardly realizing that anyone else had been behind him. He handed one of the boys to Buster. The other boy began to cry, so Winona reached out to hold him again and calmed the baby by rocking him back and forth in her arms. Jake said, "I'll find her, Winona. I promise."

They continued walking over debris toward the front of the school. Jake stopped and turned to Buster. "Will you take my wife and the boys back to the house in my truck? I need to start helping the others and find my daughter." Buster assured Jake that he would. Jake took Buster aside and asked him not to leave Winona alone, and Buster agreed.

As Winona and Buster began to walk in the direction of the parking lot, Winona abruptly turned back to Jake and told him, "We can take Edwina's car. You'll need your truck later to bring Lataine home." Jake gave Winona a puzzled look. Winona then told him about finding Edwina and four-year-old Tommy. Jake headed off in the direction of the workers who had begun using crowbars, pipes and shovels to lift rubble, free victims and listen for signs of life.

In 1937 people often left their keys in the car, and Winona knew Edwina was in the habit of doing so. Buster escorted Winona to the car and drove her home. On the way, they were met by countless ambulances, fire rescue trucks and police vehicles that were passing endless lines of cars headed in the direction of the school. Winona knew that Glenn's father, Mr. Belcher, was likely among the oilfield workers that were heading to the school in droves from the surrounding area. She knew what he would find when he arrived at the school grounds, but could do nothing to prepare him.

Her neighborhood looked eerily abandoned, except for a group of mothers who were standing at the entrance to the lease, hoping their children would be on the next school bus. There were no children walking or playing outside. No one was sitting on their front porches or working in their lawns or gardens, and most driveways were empty. Winona and Buster parked Edwina's car in front of the Belcher home across the street and left a note for Mr. Belcher that read, *Brought your car to get home.*

Tommy is alive and was taken to the hospital. Will talk soon. --Winona McQuaid.

Meanwhile, back at the school, Jake noticed one of his men holding two young girls by the hand that he had found standing outside near a window with a classmate and their teacher. The teacher had pushed both girls out of a broken window, and then crawled out herself. The girls were almost frozen with fear, not knowing what to do. As they got closer to Jake, he recognized one of the girls as Lataine's friend Ruby, who had gone with her and Betty to the movies on Saturday afternoons.

Jake asked his daughter's friend, "Are you OK, Sweetheart?"

Ruby could barely speak. She managed to give Jake a faint "Yes, sir." Jake asked her if she had seen his daughter. She was able to tell him that she had seen Lataine, Betty and Glenn earlier that day.

"Where were they when this happened?" asked Jake.

"Lataine and Glenn were going to Mrs. Wright's class, but I had to go to a different class. Betty went to the auditorium." Ruby did not fully understand why Jake was asking her these questions and asked him, "Where is Lataine?"

"We haven't found her yet, but we're still looking. Where is Mrs. Wright's class?" Jake was trying to figure out where to begin searching.

Ruby looked up toward what remained of the second story of the demolished school building. The principal, Mr. Waggoner, was standing below it with raised arms, instructing an injured child who was trapped on a ledge above him to jump into his arms. The top floor walls were missing entirely. Ruby said, "It used to be over there." She pointed into the air to the right of the tallest remaining section of the building. Jake looked above a huge pile of mangled debris where one of the three wings leading away from the building's facade once stood.

When Jake realized where she was pointing, his countenance faded into anxious despair. He whispered, "Thank you, Sweetheart. Arnie here will make sure you get home safe, OK?"

Jake and his worker nodded at one another as Ruby and her classmate continued to be escorted toward the parking lot where they were handed along to emergency medical workers. Some of the injured victims were being loaded into a bread truck that had been emptied to transport patients to the nearest available hospital or clinic.

Jake began walking in the direction Ruby had pointed, toward a large heap that was layered over by row after row of scattered roofing tiles and bricks. He joined a group of workers trying to dislodge a section of roof that had collapsed. On the opposite side of the heap was a deeper section that seemed to extend below ground level.

The explosion had blasted away the earth itself, leaving a crater that was partially refilled by falling debris.

Like the other men who wasted no time digging into the collapsed structure, Jake did what he knew how to do best. He worked as hard as he could as fast as he could and only gave an order when a coordinated effort was needed to get the job done.

Rescue and recovery efforts would continue into the night. As equipment and personnel poured into the disaster area from around the state and beyond, the nation and the world listened for any signs of life that might yet be resurrected from the unhallowed mass graves that remained buried under tons of ash and rubble.

16. Calls for Help

In just minutes following the explosion, every roadway for miles around was full of cars, back to back, trying to get to the school. Most of the cars were filled with panicked parents. As word of the disaster spread, thousands of automobiles blocked the highways leading into the community. The state police and American Legionnaires rushed to the scene and took charge, but crowds estimated at more than 5,000 soon threatened to overwhelm the volunteer workers. The curious and would-be rescuers were elbow to elbow with parents of children who were still missing. Though the onlookers were united by hope and the best of intentions, they were making it impossible for rescue vehicles to get to the scene. To remedy the situation, the Texas Governor ordered the Texas National Guard to the school to keep the roads to the site open.

Judson Woolley was Mr. Mac's nephew. He lived a mile further from the school down the same road that ran in front of Mr. Mac's house. Mr. Mac's family saw Judson running down the road towards them. He ran into their front yard with everyone yelling to him, but never said a word. He ran in the front door of their house, straight through it, and out the back door into the woods before returning to his home that evening. He would remain in shock and sit silently for weeks afterward. Judson never remembered what happened that day or how he survived to run those seven miles to get home. John Dow also miraculously survived to tell his account of what he saw that triggered the blast, but could never remember how he escaped death.

By 3:20 pm, immediately after the blast, calls had been placed to the Central Telephone Office, and the band director at the London School, Mr. Sory, headed for Overton. At 3:40 pm, he rushed into the Western Union office in Overton and exclaimed, **"The London School is blown to bits, hundreds killed and injured! Get help!"** No one knew at this time how many lives had been lost. The mayor of Henderson soon arrived on the scene, quickly surveyed the devastation, and rushed back to Henderson to set up a relief headquarters at the Chamber of Commerce office.

Without hesitation, approximately 1,500 oilfield workers rushed to the blast site. They were joined by 500 more able-bodied men and women who worked relentlessly for hours, looking for bodies and any evidence of identification. Many were afraid they would find their own missing children who had been inside the school when it blew up.

The oilfield workers were delayed at least an hour by the tallest wall that was still standing. It was tottering and seemed ready to collapse at any moment. Before they could search for the children below it, the wall had to be pulled down. When it fell, the main telephone line was cut in two. Heavy equipment and hydraulic jacks were brought in to remove the large concrete slabs that were covering so many crushed classrooms. Workers continued to work feverishly, recovering bodies from the debris using torches, hand picks and everything available to them.

A growing number of survivors soon began gathering at the football field. An area by the school's fence was used to begin laying out the dead, and another area was designated for those who were seriously injured. Peach baskets were handed out for rescue workers to use in collecting personal items for identification. A "basket brigade" of sorts was soon organized by rescue workers to transport debris from the rubble to another area where it could be dumped and examined. One mother had a heart attack and died when she learned that only part of her daughter's face had been recovered.

Besides those who were robbed of life, hundreds more were robbed of their offspring that day. Although fearing the worst, bus driver Lonnie Barber managed to safely deliver his grade school passengers before returning to the school. As the children departed the bus, frantic mothers questioned them, asking if they had seen their own children. When the last passenger departed the bus at the end of his two-hour route, Lonnie returned to the scene and immediately started helping dig for survivors. Many of the rescuers already had bloody hands and knees by the time he returned to the school.

Twenty-eight miles away in Tyler, Sarah McClendon, a $10-a-week reporter for the Tyler Courier-Times, returned to work from the beauty shop that afternoon to find a stunned newspaper office that had just learned of the explosion. She grabbed her photographer and was the first reporter on the scene. She found Mr. Shaw, the school superintendent, staggering and clutching his head wound, crying **"Oh my God, those poor children."** Later she would write, *It was like a vision from the end of the world... most of the school had, literally, vanished, leaving a rubble-littered crater to show where it had been. I found one man walking, dazed, among hundreds of bodies, mostly children, covering the ground. He managed to tell me that he was the assistant superintendent and what little else he could. I called my office in Tyler and the International News Service in Dallas just before the telephones went out. No one could phone in or out for hours.*

Years later, Sarah McClendon would become a White House correspondent and was quoted saying, "I'll never forget seeing the bones of a little girl, picked as clean as a whistle, clean as if they had been boiled... She was probably never identified. The blast literally tore the flesh from her bones."

Other reporters soon arrived on the scene to find themselves swept up in the rescue effort. Ted Hudson was working for a radio studio in Rusk County. He learned of the blast around 3:30 pm, grabbed enough equipment to go on the air, and drove to New London. He was somehow able to connect the telephone line that had torn loose from the building. He summoned doctors, nurses and others to help. He began directing rescue and clean-up efforts and would later inform ministers and singers where to go for the next funeral. Ted would stay there for the next three days and nights. His listeners were not just the anxious, grief-weary East Texans, but people throughout the world. Many of them were parents, mesmerized by what could have been their own worst nightmare. Ted Hudson once said, "As long as I had not known the broadcast was going beyond our own section, I was perfectly at ease, but when I learned we were on the national network I got a real case of 'mic fright' and turned it over to another announcer."

The explosion gave a bloody baptism to many of the 20th century's prominent journalists. A twenty-year-old Walter Cronkite was dispatched from his United Press International news office in Dallas, 125 miles west of New London. This was one of his first assignments for UPI. As soon as he received confirmation that a major story was breaking in New London, Cronkite hitched a ride on a fire department searchlight truck.

When he finally reached the scene it was dark, and rain was hampering the rescue effort. Floodlights were set up. Huge oilfield cranes were brought in to help remove the rubble. During Cronkite's radio broadcast he reportedly stated, **"Workers are climbing up and down the piles of debris like ants, instinctively going about their grim task."**

This was a tragedy of epic proportions from the perspective of this young cub reporter. Cronkite was soon joined by his UPI team that set up a news bureau in the Overton Western Union office where band director Sory had made his initial plea for help. For four days, Cronkite used a car for what little sleep he could get. He called CBS Radio in New York from a pay phone to describe the events, and they put him directly on the air each time he called.

Cronkite would later say in a local news report, "You couldn't even recognize the building. There were no walls. There was nothing left of it. There was something that looked like a roof, but it was on the ground. It had just collapsed. As we got closer and were able to park the car and get out and get up to the scene, we realized that these… tough oilfield workers with tear-stained faces, and their hands were bleeding, torn away by these jagged edges of stone and brick, and they were carrying bodies out every other minute or two."

Although Walter Cronkite would later cover World War II and the Nuremberg trials, decades later he would confess, "I did nothing in my studies nor in my life to prepare me for a story of the magnitude of that New London tragedy, nor has any story since that awful day equaled it."

At 4:15 pm, President Roosevelt was informed of the explosion and relayed the following message to the American public, *I am appalled by the news of the disaster at New London, Texas in which hundreds of school children lost their lives. I am shocked and can only hope that further information will lessen the degree of this tragedy... I have asked the Red Cross and all government agencies to stand by and render every assistance in their power to the community onto which this tragedy has come.*

Mother Frances Hospital in nearby Tyler was scheduled to open the next day, but the dedication was canceled and the hospital opened immediately. After the Overton, Kilgore and Henderson hospitals were filled to capacity with injured and dying children, a temporary hospital was set up at a church in Overton. Numerous bodies were unrecognizable, mangled and torn so badly that identification was difficult or impossible. One youngster was finally able to identify his dead brother, but only after reaching into his pocket and locating the familiar string he used to spin his prize top.

Bus driver, Lonnie Barber was just one year from retirement. Before the night was over, Lonnie would learn that he had lost his youngest son, Arden. Nevertheless, through tears of grief, he continued searching through the night for the sons and daughters of his neighbors.

Over the next few hours, aid poured in from all over. The Texas governor dispatched the Texas Rangers and the highway patrol, along with the Texas National Guard. Thirty doctors, one hundred nurses, and twenty-five embalmers arrived from Dallas, Fort Worth, Nacogdoches and Wichita Falls.

Airmen aboard five planes departed from Barksdale Field in Louisiana carrying supplies and medical personnel. Deputy sheriffs from Overton, Henderson, and Kilgore, the American Legion, the Salvation Army, the American Red Cross and even the Boy Scouts took part in rescue and recovery efforts.

A Red Cross representative who had been on the scene would later write, *Mothers sifted through the debris desperately for some proof of the identity of their children. They picked up and carried tiny scraps of gingham or corduroy, or whatever charred swatches matched what they remembered their little ones had left home wearing. Screams of recognition filled the air.*

The news of the London School explosion spread

quickly to relatives and loved ones in surrounding towns and other parts of the state.

An Empty Tomb (CS)

17. Out of the Rubble

When news of the disaster reached the town of Talco, all Humble Oil employees were told that anyone wishing to assist in the rescue effort could to go to New London. One of those employees was my grandfather, Papa Dee, who immediately went home and informed his wife and family of the news. Papa Dee and Granny decided to leave their children at home with his parents and drive there.

Mother recalled the time vividly because she had never before been left in the care of anyone other than her own parents for any length of time. Papa Dee and Granny arrived in New London near sunset and proceeded directly to the school.

When they arrived, it became immediately apparent that the rescue effort was fully underway. Emergency rescue vehicles were parked end to end, arriving and departing from the school property. Overhead lights were being set up in and around the disaster area, and it had begun to rain. Papa Dee and Granny decided to go to Jake and Winona's house first, before attempting to enter the rescue zone that was now being guarded by armed National Guardsmen.

They left the school and went directly to the McQuaid home. Even though there was no vehicle in the driveway, they knocked on the front door. Buster opened it, and Papa Dee asked him, "Is Jake or Winona here?" Buster then welcomed them into the house.

Winona was sitting on the sofa rocking one of her twin boys in her lap when she noticed her cousin. She looked up at Granny and said, "We don't know where Lataine is. Jake is at the school looking for her."

Granny immediately went over to her and put her arm around Winona's shoulders. Buster introduced himself and explained that he worked for Jake. Buster's eyes betrayed his concern for Winona and the missing girl. He took Papa Dee to one side and told him that he would prefer to be helping with the rescue, but that Jake insisted Winona not be left alone.

Granny started to talk with Winona, who couldn't contain her tears while telling Granny about her friend Edwina, finding little Tommy, and how she was so afraid for her daughter after seeing what happened to the school. Granny picked up the infant from Winona's lap and told her she was going to put him in his bed. Winona nodded and put her face in her hands, exhausted from the events of the day.

Granny told Papa Dee and Buster, "I'll stay here with Winona if you two want to go to the school and find Jake. We'll be fine. I'll make her a bite to eat and see if she will lie down." Papa Dee and Buster agreed and left the house.

When they arrived at the disaster site, armed guards were barring curiosity seekers from entering the area. Papa Dee and Buster were permitted to enter, after explaining they had come to help in the rescue effort. Papa Dee decided to assist the workers who were still loading victims for transport to the morgues in the area. Most of the injured victims had already been taken to clinics and hospitals.

Buster soon joined Jake and the other men who were working under artificial lights in the rubble. By this time, the uppermost layers of concrete and debris from the area where Ruby had pointed had been painstakingly removed using heavy-duty jacks.

Workers soon found a row of metal lockers lying scattered about that had been dislodged from the walls by the blast. Jake picked up one of the lockers. Near one remnant of a remaining wall was a blackboard. Jake read the words that were still visible on it. They seemed vaguely familiar. He recalled discussing the subject of natural resources with his daughter the night before, when she had been working on her homework. Jake began picking up more lockers, pieces of broken desks, glass and chunks of plaster for any sign that would lead him toward the daughter he was searching for.

Beneath a broken desk, Buster located a child's body. Another worker a few yards away found a boy lying beneath two steel lockers that were propped over a broken desk. Workers called for assistance to remove the bodies. Jake looked over both bodies and recognized that one was Glenn, the boy who had ridden to school with him that morning. He was lying outstretched on his back, with both hands pointing in the direction of another desk that was overturned and perched precariously at the edge of the drop-off that led down into the buried crater.

Buster reached down to wipe away the thick layer of plaster covering the boy's face that was now getting wet in the rain and noticed a trickle of blood running down Glenn's forehead. Amazingly, the boy opened both of his eyes and began to speak. Excited by the find, workers promptly helped Glenn to his feet and escorted him to the closest medical personnel. He was treated for his head wound that had left him unconscious, but apart from minor bruises, Glenn seemed alert and healthy.

Confused by what had happened, Glenn could recall nothing prior to sitting in his classroom and talking with Lataine. Soon he began asking about her and his other classmates, but no one had any answers for him.

Jake continued to work in the same area. He picked up the desk that had protected Glenn from the heavy steel lockers and falling debris. Under the bright lights that had been set up for the work to continue into the night, Jake saw something shining. He reached out for it, only to realize it was the ring his daughter had worn every day since Christmas. Jake recoiled in horror.

Buster looked over at Jake. All the color drained from his face, and Jake could only turn aside from what he had just discovered. Buster laid his handkerchief over the child's severed finger and put the ring in his pocket. Buster helped Jake climb down off the debris pile and attempted to escort him back toward the parking area. Stooping over like a wounded animal, Jake repeatedly fell to his knees. Sick and moaning, he toppled forward, landing on all fours in the slick, rain-soaked mud and ash that was everywhere. Jake McQuaid had lost all hope of ever seeing his daughter smile again.

News quickly spread about the boy who was found alive, giving new hope to those who had yet to find their children. Their searching would continue.

18. Survivors and Losses

Glenn Belcher was soon located by his father. By that time, Mr. Belcher was carefully looking over the bodies that were being lined up by the school fence. Dead students were being transported to the various morgues in the area. After having found his dead wife and learning that his son, Tommy, was safe in the hospital, Mr. Belcher was almost devoid of hope for finding Glenn alive. Their reunion was indescribably emotional.

Emergency workers on the scene were at their wits end trying to identify the bodies of the deceased. Knowing that Glenn had just been rescued from the rubble where bodies were being removed one after another, the head of the Texas National Guard medical team approached Glenn and his father.

"Sir... pardon me, Mr. Belcher. My name is Colonel Walter Pyron with the 112th Cavalry Medical Detachment of the Texas National Guard out of Mineral Wells. Understanding that I have no direct authority in this matter, I would be honored if your boy could assist us in identifying some of the students we have uncovered. We've got parents lined up all around the school trying to identify their children."

"I'm not sure we're up for that, Colonel. Glenn here took quite a blow to his head and was knocked out for some time." said Mr. Belcher. "We lost his mother and need to go find his baby brother who is in one of the hospitals."

"I understand sir. If I can be of any further assistance…"

Glenn interrupted the Colonel. "I want to help out if I can, Pa."

"I don't know, Son. Are you sure you feel up to it?"

"Yes, Pa. I haven't seen any of my friends. I'm worried about 'em. I don't know what happened when I was out, but I'm gonna be OK. We can go see Tommy when we're done here. He'll be taken good care of in the hospital until we get there. Please let me help if I can." begged Glenn.

Glenn's father told the Colonel that they would try to help, but that if the task became too difficult, he would have to take Glenn away. The Colonel agreed and asked both to follow him. Colonel Pyron was soon lifting the sheets that had been placed over the faces of victims that were being lined up beside the fence. Glenn recognized nearly all of the children, but could not provide the names for most. For others, he knew only their first name or nickname. Nevertheless, the Colonel made a note on his clipboard each time Glenn gave him any information. Many of the bodies were marred beyond recognition. He identified Ollie from the corduroy jacket he wore everyday, and thought the boy next to him might be his friend, Billy, but he was unsure.

"Colonel Walter," asked Glenn. "Would you mind looking in his back pocket? If this is Billy, you should find his cap rolled up there." Colonel Pyron searched the dead boy's pockets to find what Glenn had feared. Glenn continued down the line of sheeted corpses and soon recognized Mary's beautiful face with her auburn hair. Glenn soon became somewhat overwhelmed, and his daddy became concerned.

"Son, you don't have to keep doing this. These kids are all with God now. There's no need for you to continue. We've both had more than our share of upset today." said Glenn's father.

"I need to find Lataine if I can, Daddy. Please let me keep helping the Colonel for a while longer." Mr. Belcher acquiesced to his son's insistence, but told Colonel Pyron he didn't think they could continue much longer. The Colonel said he understood, but that Glenn was providing some very much needed information for the children's families. Glenn soon identified his classmates, Kenneth and Helen, along with four others from Mrs. Wright's class.

At some point, the task of seeing more and more of his friends and classmates must have become more than Glenn could take. He began to hyperventilate and started running ahead of Colonel Pyron and his father, moving from one body to another, pulling sheets off the faces of each victim, laying it back down and moving to the next one as fast as he could. His father yelled for Glenn to stop. Glenn froze in place, staring at the next body he was about to unveil.

"Tell me what's going on, Glenn." demanded his father.

"I need to find Lataine, Daddy! I can't find her anywhere."

Colonel Pyron asked Glenn, "Can you describe her to me, Glenn?"

"Yes, sir. She was at my house last night and we were at school all day. I rode with her daddy this morning and she helped him drive through the lease. She's about an inch shorter than me with light blue eyes and has long hair that turns blond in the sun. She was wearing a pink dress with a white collar the last time I saw her, and wears a gold ring with a gold rose on it."

Colonel Pyron looked at the ground to collect his thoughts before breaking the news to young Glenn. "I'm so sorry, Glenn. Lataine's daddy identified her just after they freed you from the rubble. I hate to be the one to tell you this, but she's gone."

Glenn's heart sank. He hung his head and began to weep as his father wrapped a gentle arm around his shoulders. Colonel Pyron told Mr. Belcher, "It's time to take your boy away from this place, Mr. Belcher. Thank you both for your assistance. I know this has been difficult. I will make a note of your son's admirable service." He turned to Glenn and said, "Thank you, Sir. You should be proud, Glenn Belcher."

The Colonel reached out to shake Glenn's hand. Glenn could not immediately look up at him, but nevertheless extended his hand. The Colonel remained standing at attention until the boy finally looked him in the eyes. When he finally did, Colonel Walter B. Pyron saluted the young man, turned in military fashion, and proceeded back to his medical team to pass along the information he had obtained.

Glenn matured quickly that night, sooner than most. The nightmares of this day would haunt him for years to come, but the fonder memories of his mother, the friends that he had lost forever, and his first love would provide him the inner strength he needed to carry on.

Glenn's friend and summertime co-worker, Joe Bo Kerce, was now safe at his home, having run three miles from the school to escape the devastation and commotion he had witnessed. He had a brother and an older sister who were also at the school. Both barely escaped with their lives.

Joe Bo had helped his English teacher, a member of his church, escape through a narrow opening from the demolished, caved in classroom where they were when the school exploded. He had seen his classmate, Billy Hall, with a big gash on the side of his face.

Another one of Joe Bo's classmates who survived was less fortunate. Years later, Joe Bo would eventually tell his story by saying, "My little playmate, Johnny Duke, had his head popped open and to this day he is walking around with a steel plate in his head." Vera's family had once lived directly behind Johnny Duke. Vera and Johnny's sister, Opal, were best of friends for several years.

Joe Bo's stepfather, a welder for Humble Oil and former president of the London School Board, was returning home from work when the school blew up. Joe Bo described what his father had done. "He was coming from the fields and it happened just when he was coming by the school," said Joe Bo. "He was driving one of those Humble welding trucks, tore a school fence right down and started to work." Joe Bo was not exactly sure how long his father helped at the scene, but believed he remained there for 24 hours. Like many survivors and rescuers in years to come, the father rarely spoke about his experience. Joe Bo said, "For a long time, he was very tight-lipped on stuff like that."

Years later, Joe Bo would still be removing tiny bits of concrete from his skull, but he avoided any future discussion or reminisces. He described how he coped with his trauma following the tragedy. "No words can describe or illustrate what happened there... I don't want to think about the past. It's done and it's over with. I prefer to think about the glorified days ahead."

Before the explosion, H. G. White had just returned to his desk after asking his 5th grade math teacher, Miss Lena Hunt, to assist him with a problem. Then he began working on his multiplication tables. "I looked out the south window and something caught my eye... it just felt like somebody slapped me upside the head." recalled White. Five boys and three girls survived out of the thirty-two students in his classroom. He was one of those boys. His teacher, Miss Hunt, was also killed. Another teacher found him while searching for survivors in the rubble. "The plaster was about an inch thick. It covered me up." H. G. said, "When she stepped, she fell into me and saw I was alive. She reached down and pulled me up. I wasn't knocked out, so I can remember every squeak..." Although he sustained head injuries in the blast, H. G. felt blessed to be alive. He later stated in an interview, "I should pay some debt to somebody, because I was fortunate, real fortunate to walk away..."

Approximately 500 students and 40 teachers were at the school at the time of the explosion. Only 130 of those would escape without serious injury. Most, but not all, of the additional parents and pre-school children were protected inside the gym. The earliest death tolls were underestimated. They included 120 boys, 156 girls, 4 male teachers, and 12 female teachers. The remains of some were never recovered. Six more dead were accounted for in the days that followed. Of the 112 critically injured victims, 13 would die shortly thereafter. Extended hospital stays would be necessary for at least 39 students.

Rescuers continued working throughout the night in the rain and mud. Around 2,000 tons of debris were picked up and hauled away. Concrete slabs were broken up. Tangled steel was cut with torches. Smaller fragments of rubble that had to be shoveled were carried off in small baskets and carefully emptied under the floodlights to avoid overlooking a hand or foot or any torn portion of a body.

Buildings in the neighboring communities of Henderson, Overton, Kilgore and as far away as Tyler and Longview were converted into makeshift morgues to house the enormous number of bodies. Everything from family cars to delivery trucks served as hearses and ambulances. Frantic parents continued searching, viewing torn and mangled corpses to try and identify their missing children.

When daylight arrived, seventeen hours following the explosion, the entire site had been leveled. However, work in the area and official investigations at the disaster site continued for days. For the parents who had to bury their children and carry on with their lives, the days that followed were no less heart-wrenching.

The poem that follows was written by one of the youngest survivors of this tragedy and chillingly expresses what so many who were devastated experienced and were feeling on that night and the following day.

COLD MORNING, 1937

The night of the disaster, no one slept.
Sirens ripped the darkness with doom.
Dogs howled back. After the bodies
were found, we tried sleep,
stared at the ceiling, fixed by memories
we could never escape or soon describe.

Exhaustion loosened our grip on consciousness,
we slipped into a dark pool, lay floating
face down below the surface, until
the gray pool merged with gray dawn.

We rose, forcing our leaden feet
to the terrible task: caskets, the unctuous
minister, the exhausted emergency worker.

In a garage beside the mortuary,
makeshift tables held the remnants of lives,
shrouded in bloody sheets.

Rituals were omitted. No neighbors stood
in doorways bearing plates of cake.
Those not bereaved avoided our eyes,
terrible as gorgons.

Yesterday's March morning warmed
to the trills of mockingbirds. Gulf breezes
rushing inland tossed new bluebonnets.
Today is a cottonmouth under a cold stone.

-- Carolyn Jones Frei

The Days After

19. A Community Devastated

Granny and Papa Dee remained at the McQuaid home for the next couple of weeks caring for Winona, Jake and the twin boys. Papa Dee volunteered by day helping workers dig fresh graves at the Pleasant Hill Cemetery near New London, where most of the bodies were buried. Granny helped the families they knew in New London by cooking meals and assisting with the funeral arrangements for Glenn's mother, Edwina.

Glenn and Ruby attended Betty's funeral that was held at their church. The pianist and choir director performed the song *Danny Boy* in Betty's honor.

Glenn and his father also joined the McQuaid family at the funeral service for Lataine that was held at the Crim Funeral Home in Henderson. Her meager remains were buried in a family plot at the Kingsbury Cemetery three hundred miles away between Luling and Seguin. For helping her and Jake to get through the long days following the tragedy, Winona gave Granny the small gold ring that Lataine had worn every day.

The London School explosion killed 298 students and teachers instantly, according to the Handbook of Texas Online. The death toll was officially recorded as 311, making it the worst catastrophe to take place in a U.S. school building. Some estimates that tried to account for students who were never found and some who lingered even longer, listed the actual number of dead to be as high as 325.

The event was truly an explosion heard round the world. Leaders across the globe, including Eleanor Roosevelt, sent telegrams and letters of sympathy. Correspondences were received from as far away as Japan, Spain, France, Warsaw and Belgrade to pay respect to the survivors of the East Texas community. Politically, America was at odds with Germany, but the German Chancellor, Adolf Hitler, also cabled his condolences to President Franklin D. Roosevelt with this message, *I want to assure your Excellency of the German people's sincere sympathy.*

One can only wonder what thoughts were evoked by this event in the mind of the man who would intentionally slaughter millions of innocent men, women and children in the years that followed. It had only been three and a half months since Hitler had made it mandatory for all young Germans over age nine (excluding Jews) to join the Nazi Hitler Youth organization. Parents who prevented their children from joining the Hitler Youth were already being subjected to heavy prison sentences. Two years later he would invade Poland and begin ordering mass executions of civilians. The world's awareness of the Holocaust in Europe would soon follow.

The main building on the London School campus was completely destroyed. However, the gymnasium was soon converted into multiple classrooms. The usable buildings that remained standing were modified, and new tents were set up. Classes resumed ten days later following Easter Sunday.

The Texas Governor and state legislators called for an immediate military investigation into the cause of the explosion. A special committee of the Texas Legislature and the United States Bureau of Mines also conducted investigations. Engineers even drilled all over the school campus and found no seepage of gas from any underground source.

One of the maintenance men testified that he had entered the building's crawlspace at 10 o'clock in the morning, five hours before the explosion, and had even lit some matches inside it to find his way in the dark. However, he had entered at the extreme south end of the building, at least 200 yards away from where the explosion originated.

Eighteen sticks of dynamite that were stored in a lumber room under the auditorium stage went through the explosion intact. Apparently, that discovery was not viewed as a cause for any significant concern at the time.

Official reports concluded that no one was at fault for the explosion, but experts from the Bureau of Mines determined that the connections to the residue gas line that the maintenance men had installed were faulty and led to gas accumulation beneath the building. Public pressure led to demands that the government immediately begin regulating engineering practices because of the faulty gas line connections that fueled the disaster. The Texas Legislature met in an emergency session and passed the Engineering Registration Act that established a mandatory legal requirement for gas connections, gauges and control valves to be installed by licensed personnel.

When the explosion occurred, Carolyn Jones and her close friend, Barbara Moore, had been practicing spelling words for an upcoming spelling bee with their teacher, Mrs. Sory, the band director's wife. All three escaped from the rubble that was their classroom. Hours later, Carolyn's sister and uncle were located in makeshift morgues.

On March 25th, nine-year-old survivor, Carolyn Jones, spoke to the Texas Legislature about the importance of safety in schools. (Her speech is reprinted in its entirety in the Appendix.) Her words so moved the assembly that the state legislature immediately passed a law mandating the odor agent, mercaptan (a sulfur-containing organic compound), be added to all natural gas. The strong, foul-smelling odor of the chemical makes leaks quickly detectable. The practice quickly spread worldwide. Now a retired school teacher, Carolyn Jones Frei lives in Lewiston, Idaho. Barbara Moore Page lives in Weatherford, Texas.

There were 80 lawsuits filed, but no legal action was taken. A lawsuit was also brought against the school district and the company that provided the natural gas for the school. The court ruled that neither could be held responsible.

Superintendent W. C. Shaw, who lost a child of his own in the explosion, was forced to resign as rumors of a plan to lynch him began to surface. Several parents began carrying side arms, even at public meetings. The oil companies transferred some families out of the area for their own safety.

The Texas Rangers surrounded the house of Jack Kern, the President of the School Board, to protect him and his family from angry parents who had lost their children. During the aftermath, Mr. Kern had helped at the disaster site for hours. Kern's daughter, Priscilla, was one of the students who performed the *Mexican Hat Dance,* along with my Aunt Vera and Mollie Ward, during the PTA meeting on March 18th. My Aunt Vera vividly remembered Priscilla and her mother, because they attended the same church in New London. Recently, my aunt became amused while recalling that Mrs. Kern would often embroidery her daughter's clothing during their minister's sermons.

The 1937 high school graduation ceremony at the London School was held only two months after the catastrophe. It was a very somber affair. There were more vacant seats than filled ones in the senior class, and those who had perished were remembered. The entire town was still in a state of shock. A new school was completed in 1939 on the same property, directly behind the destroyed building. It continued to be known as the London School until 1965, when the name was changed.

The event devastated a community and wiped away another layer of innocence from the American landscape. The tragedy held a special terror. On the fiftieth anniversary of the explosion in 1987, United Press International reporter for the Los Angeles Times, William H. Inman wrote, *It was selective death, the last and cruelest plague of Moses.*

Afterward, a long silence permeated the town of New London, Texas. Unlike today, when individuals grieve openly following a disaster and their healing process is often viewed by reporters and television cameras, the bereaved family members in and around New London buried their dead and wept privately. Then they began trying to put their lives back together as best they could. After this horrific calamity, the brilliant shine of effervescent hope that had been so prevalent in New London was no longer there. A sign at the edge of town explained why. It read simply, "WE LOVE OUR CHILDREN."

Although Elsie had remained safe in the gym with her mother at the time of the explosion, Kenneth and Elsie's father would have a more difficult time coping with the death of his son than many other parents, knowing that he had forced him to attend school that day.

Glenn's younger brother, Tommy, was located by his father on the day after the explosion and released from the hospital where he had been treated for minor injuries. Glenn's father soon moved back to his childhood home in the Houston area, where Glenn and Tommy were introduced to family members and cousins their age that they had never met. Mr. Belcher remarried and had a daughter by his second wife. They named her Edwina. Some of Glenn's friends and classmates who survived remained in New London. Vera Hendrix and Jo Bo Kerce were two of those whose final stories remain to be told.

An Empty Tomb (CS)

20. Memories and Mysteries

Glenn's friend and co-worker, Claude Joseph "Joe Bo" Kerce, remained in New London and picked cotton during his boyhood summers. At school, he played football, baseball and basketball. Joe Bo reported on his athletic performance by saying, "I wasn't worth a dime..." Joe Bo became the marching band drum major in his junior year, and graduated from the rebuilt London School.

When America entered World War II, Joe Bo got his parent's permission to join the Navy. After six weeks of intensive training in Corpus Christi, he was assigned aboard a destroyer, the USS Fred T. Berry. He participated in the Pacific theater during the invasions of the Marianas and Tinian. After the war, he worked for Humble, Mobil and Magnolia Oil Companies. Joe Bo eventually moved to Dallas and worked for Braniff Airlines as a maintenance man and later at GTE, where he retired in 1991. In 2010, Joe Bo was still with his wife of 55 years in Desoto, Texas. Together they raised three children, and so far have two granddaughters, one grandson and a great-grandson.

Not having read Joe Bo's account of the events surrounding this tragedy until this year in 2011, my Aunt Vera recently wrote, *In Joe Bo's memo, he mentioned taking music from Mrs. Lancaster and that she always had a coke in her class. I also remember this and that she always put an aspirin in it. Back then, cokes contained cocaine, so we kids thought she was experiencing a high.*

Joe Bo's playmate, Johnny Duke, who had survived with a steel plate in his head, eventually married a girl in Vera's class. Writing about Johnny Duke later in life, Vera reported, *They had either a son or grandson (not sure which) who was born mentally ill. One day when Johnny was sitting downstairs at his home, reading the newspaper, the boy came down the stairs and shot him (Johnny Duke) in the head. Isn't it strange how 75 years have passed, memories had dimmed, and a memo from a survivor brought it all flooding back?*

The people in and around New London, Texas continued to suffer collectively for decades from what we now recognize as post-traumatic stress. Almost forty years later in the mid-1970's, small groups of survivors and family members of the deceased began holding private reunions. The reunions served as a healing process for many who were still carrying unspoken grief and "survivor guilt". There, they could talk about their experiences during and after the explosion, and amid their tearful recollections, begin to heal. The reunions will continue until there are no more survivors.

H. G. White would meet at the reunion of survivors in New London, Texas in 2011 and tell the story of his brush with death 74 years after the event took place. He is now retired and lives in Lindale, Texas.

Although still paralyzed from his swimming injury that happened prior to the explosion, Billy's relative, Danny Miller, was still alive in the 1970's and being cared for by Granny's sister, Johnnie Marie, in a nursing home near Luling where she worked.

Another survivor of the explosion, Helen Sillick looked back on the event as if it was a dream. "I remember being thrown up into the air like a toy, looking around me and seeing the parts of buildings floating in the air with me. *I'm up above the school*, I think to myself. I can see people walking around, screaming. I keep turning and spinning. Then darkness."

Myrtle Faye Hayes distinctly remembered a daily ritual in the classrooms that began to take place a considerable period of time before the day of the explosion. It involved the need to open the windows and get fresh air into the rooms to counteract the dizziness and burning eyes that was almost always present. In hindsight, it became obvious to her that the explosive gas had been slowly collecting under the floor for days, if not weeks.

After the explosion, Myrtle recalled a tearful reunion with her father, who was frantically clearing away rubble looking for her. By the time she was found, her father and her mother already knew that her brother, William, had been killed in the explosion. Now retired from a long career in business, Myrtle lives in Longview, Texas.

Some people believe the explosion was an act of sabotage. Twenty-four years later, on July 18, 1961, a former student of the London School, William Estel Benson, sat in a police station in Oklahoma City while a photographer snapped his photo. Benson had been arrested for questioning about a $38 robbery. He was a convicted burglar and a mental patient who had spent many of his adult years in mental institutions, reportedly trying to deal with his grief. His sister, fourteen-year-old Betty Lou, had died in the explosion.

William Estel had helped his stepfather install the school's plumbing system. "My stepfather owned a pipe yard, and I worked with him," he said. "I knew plenty about oil and gas pipes, but I didn't really intend to kill anybody." He said he unscrewed gas pipes beneath the school, hoping to "run up a gas bill". He said he was angry at the time, because the principal had scolded him for smoking. Although Benson retracted his story a few days later by saying his confession was "all a hoax", he had managed to divulge accurate details that had never before been made public, including specifications about the gas pipes he claimed to have sabotaged. Lie detector tests given to him at the time were inconclusive. William Benson is now deceased.

A seemingly countless number of tragic, personal stories continue to be recalled, told and retold. However, the number of people who were actually there to witness the events of that fateful day in 1937 diminishes every year. Soon, all we will have left are what has been recorded of their collective and individual reports.

Vera Hendrix, Lataine's neighborhood friend, would remain in New London until her senior year, then move to Talco with her family. Although Vera and my Uncle Gerald can be seen in a photo of the London School band standing only two people apart, they never knew each other until she moved to Talco. There, they met and married. After they married, her parents became best of friends with Granny and Papa Dee. They even vacationed together and traveled across America to visit places like the Grand Canyon and the giant redwood forests in California. As my first cousins' grandparents, the Hendrix's were like another set of grandparents to me. Growing up as a child, I always referred to them as Papa and Granny Hendrix.

My Uncle Gerald would eventually find relative success in the oil business working for a small, independent oil company. At the time of his retirement, he had become vice president of the company. For three and a half years, Gerald had been in the same class as Lataine. Mother told us that had they not moved away from New London when they did (a mere six weeks before the tragedy), her brother would likely have never had an opportunity to finish school, get married or raise my first cousins with whom I was very close growing up.

My cousins grew up like my siblings and me, having been nurtured in a large extended family with Texas roots going back for nearly two centuries. My Aunt Vera, now retired, lives in Victoria, Texas. Her skills as an editor of published literature and her personal story of survival were utilized in preparing this book for publication.

When J. W. McQuaid died in 1963, he was laid to rest beside his daughter's grave. Lataine's mother, Winona, passed away in 2008 at the age of one hundred and three. She was buried in the same family plot between the two of them. Lataine's younger brothers, Dale and Gale, are still living in Texas.

Buster Nugent continued to learn everything he could about the oil business and kept in touch with Jake McQuaid throughout the years that followed Lataine's death. Eventually he struck out on his own and started his own independent oil company business. After Jake died, Buster sold his business and banked a tidy sum. Then, as sort of a semi-retirement plan, he partnered up with some other oil men who had also worked for Jake over the years.

They owned a small family-owned oil business in Luling. I was first introduced to a sixty-year-old Buster during my first day on the job when I took that temporary summer position between college semesters. I thought it odd at the time, but my first task that day was to climb an aluminum ladder to the roof of their office building while Buster looked on. I must have passed the test, because afterward he told me I could get in the work truck and head to the job site with the rest of the crew. I think he probably had a lot more to say when his new employees failed that initial test.

The next day Buster started calling me *Piney Woods*. We were taking a break from the hundred degree heat beneath a shade tree next to a watermelon patch, while enjoying one of the lease owner's ripe watermelons that we had gleaned from his field. When I asked him why he called me that, Buster asked me if I hadn't been raised in East Texas. He said he had been around Texas so long that he could tell which part of it a man was raised... just by listening to him speak. When I told him he was correct, and that I was raised around Talco, his stories about Jake and the times they worked together just kept on coming. He never once mentioned the explosion at the London School that summer. After almost 40 years, it was still too difficult a subject for him to talk about.

Buster and his wife also ministered for one of the local church congregations. When my grandparents eventually came up in one of our conversations, he immediately recognized their names and made me promise to invite Granny to visit his church, but to my knowledge she never did. I can only wonder how many suppressed their memories of that awful time in the spring of 1937.

Papa Dee and Granny rarely mentioned the death of their first daughter, Mildred, or what they experienced during their brief return to New London to bury the dead and offer solace to the living. Like Buster, I believe their memories of that time must have always been too painful to discuss. It would seem that such was the case with most who were there.

Papa Dee would die suddenly from a heart stroke at age 64. By then, he and Granny had moved back to the Luling area where their extended family lived. Granny would never marry again. She would live another 32 years, finally passing away in her bed in 1997 at the age of 90. Before she died, Granny left a small, antique jewelry box to her only remaining child. The box contained that small gold ring that Mother had once shared on a forgotten Christmas day to simply brighten the eyes and heart of her beloved cousin, Lataine.

Mother told us that on the night of the tragedy, after Jake had found his daughter's remains, Buster kept walking with Jake until they found Papa Dee. Then they escorted Jake back to their car. When Jake was able to speak, he told Buster to show the ring they had found to Papa Dee. Jake said, "Dee, please tell me this isn't the ring you bought for my baby girl."

Buster reached into his pocket, pulled out the gold ring and handed it to Papa Dee, who said, "I wish I could do that Jake, but it looks like the same one."

Mother's story of Lataine, along with her ring that had been stored away in its small case for more than seven decades, still reverberates with my daughter and me. On the day we were going through Granny's old Bible and Mother returned to her living room carrying the small jewelry box, she removed the small gold ring, examined it closely and said, "You can still make out where the tiny rose sat on the top of it here."

Mother soon recalled the inscription engraved on Lataine's gravestone that reads, *The Rose Still Grows Beyond the Wall*. It is from the following poem that expressed the sentiment of Lataine's mother and father when they were grieving her loss.

The Rose Still Grows Beyond the Wall

Near a shady wall a rose once grew,
Budded and blossomed in God's free light,
Watered and fed by the morning dew,
Shedding it's sweetness day and night.

As it grew and blossomed fair and tall,
Slowly rising to loftier height,
It came to a crevice in the wall
Through which there shone a beam of light.

Onward it crept with added strength
With never a thought of fear or pride,
It followed the light through the crevice's length
And unfolded itself on the other side.

The light, the dew, the broadening view
Were found the same as they were before,
And it lost itself in beauties new,
Breathing it's fragrance more and more.

Shall claim of death cause us to grieve
And make our courage faint and fall?
Nay! Let us faith and hope receive--
The rose still grows beyond the wall,

Scattering fragrance far and wide
Just as it did in days of yore,
Just as it did on the other side,
Just as it will forever-more.

A rose once grew where all could see,

sheltered beside a garden wall,
And as the days passed swiftly by,
it spread its branches, straight and tall...

One day, a beam of light shone through
a crevice that had opened wide
The rose bent gently toward its warmth
then passed beyond to the other side.

Now, you who deeply feel its loss,
be comforted - the rose blooms there-
its beauty even greater now,
nurtured by God's loving care. --A.L. Frink

Mother looked down and shook her head slowly from side to side, telling us again how beautiful Lataine was and how pretty she looked with her hair all done up in curls. She said, "I told Lataine that Christmas when I gave her this ring that only princesses ever got to wear anything that special. She never took it off, just like she promised. It was still on her finger when her daddy found it."

My daughter whispered to her grandmother that if it would be okay, she would like to keep the ring to remind her of Mother's stories from that day.

Mother said, "Here you are, Sweetheart... maybe one day you will tell her story to your own grandchildren."

My daughter placed the ring back into its antique box and said, "I'll keep it safe for you, Mimi."

I asked Mother if she would like to visit Lataine's grave when we met in Luling for the family reunion. She said she would. My daughter suggested we plant a rose bush beside her grave when we went. We did that this fall, accompanied by my brother, his son and my cousins Patsy and Jimmy.

A large granite cenotaph (a Greek word meaning "empty tomb") sits on the median of State Highway 42 in New London across from the school property. It commemorates the 1937 disaster and serves as a memorial to the teachers and students who died that perilous day almost 75 years ago. It depicts twelve life-size figures, representing children coming to school, bringing gifts and handing in homework to two teachers. The massive granite block weighs twenty tons and is supported by two monolithic granite columns with fluted sides. These twenty feet high columns rise from a granite platform which is reached on two sides by granite steps. Overall the monument is thirty-two feet high. Around the inside of the base are the individual names of those who died in the London School on March 18, 1937.

The New London Museum is located across the highway. Its curator, Mollie Ward, is an explosion survivor. She was ten years old at the time and was one of the girls who participated in the dance class performance prior to the PTA meeting in the gym that afternoon. She watched from a bus window as the New London school shook with a deafening bellow, then collapsed into a heap of bricks and dust and broken bodies. Recalling the tragedy, she said in an interview, "It's something that scars your mind--the screams, the cries--like some horrible disease you just can't shake."

Filled with artifacts, the museum is devoted to preserving the history of the students and teachers who perished in the explosion and to accurately portray the events of that fateful day. There one can find a book of memories containing the photos and descriptions of the children whose lives and futures were sacrificed upon an alter of ignorance and fatal mistakes. The poem that follows was written by survivor Carolyn Jones and describes her recollections upon examining this book of memories.

MEMORY BOOK

One muggy afternoon the students sat
for their last school pictures. In the air
from the photographer's fan
the children's hair blows to the left.

When I open the Memory Book,
dead schoolmates assume weight,
dimension. The faculty comes first
in death, knowing, dignified,
The school secretary wears a secret
smile, planning the wedding
that never came. Seniors parade
in caps and gowns, diplomas
never signed. On the yellowing
pages for primary school, wisps
of hair slip from clips and ribbons,
bangs hang unevenly.

The names are regional: Iva Jo,
Sybil, Glendell, Lataine. Boys in
their father's ties never inherited
their names. From freckled faces
clear eyes gaze, searching fate
in the camera's lens, composing
historic ovals memorized
by grieving parents.

Billy wears his skullcap, chin up,
feisty as always. Tall Ollie is shy.
The twins are separate on the page,
though never in life or death. The best

dressed girl wears her best dress.

They know the final mystery.
But we who survive memorialize
the pain, the loss of trust, another
slaughter of the innocents.

-- Carolyn Jones Frei

Many things have changed since the explosion took its toll back then. Some of those changes insure that every one of us is now safer in our homes, businesses and schools. If you visit the museum in New London, Texas on a typical day, you can often sense the faint, familiar smell of sulfides that are continually added to the natural gas wells in the nearby oilfields. It sometimes drifts invisibly through the air in this small Texas oilfield town, reminding everyone around these parts of the true cause of a tragedy that changed our world.

An Empty Tomb (CS)

APPENDIX

Billy Capps' Story

My great grandfather was the night watchman at the time of the London School explosion. His full name was William Crawford McClelland. He went by Will & some called him Mr. Mac. He had a hundred acre farm approximately five and a half miles from the school. I know because I grew up there. He died when I was nine. I heard the stories all my life from my family. My full name is William Earl Capps, I was named after him. He had a wife named Mary (Eliza) Sartain. They were known to the family as Papa & Mammy. They had four daughters... Addie, Florine (my grandmother), Willie Mae, & Avis. My grandmother had two daughters, Betty & Ann (my mother). Grandmother lived at the house when the school blew. They were all home (Grandmother was divorced). In fact, Mother was four years old & had climbed up in a tree in the yard. When the school exploded, it shook her out & gashed her arm open; she would carry a scar the rest of her life as a reminder of that day. Papa was plowing in the field with his mule when it happened. They could see it go up in the air from that far & farther. My grandmother, Florine Richardson used to tell me that she could swear she saw what appeared to be body parts (arms, legs, etc) as the explosion topped the trees. Whether she did or thought she did, I don't know. I just know growing up, I can't recall her lying or even exaggerating about anything. There was a crossroads in front of their old white bungalow, four oil roads full of cars, back to back, trying to get to the school. I don't know how they knew it was the school, but it was parents all in a panic in those cars.

One of the strangest things (and there were many) that happened at Papa's house was a while after the explosion. Mammy's sister's boy, Judson Woolley, lived a mile farther from the school down the same road as Papa. He was at school when it exploded. How he escaped death, he never remembered, but my family standing outside watching the people struggle to move in the traffic saw a boy running down the road towards them; it was Judson. He ran into the yard with every one yelling to him, but he never said a word as he ran into the front door of the large bungalow & out the back, cutting through the woods instead of the road, then running another mile home. He would sit and not utter a word for a couple of weeks, as he remained in shock. When asked about the incident in his latter years, he never remembered what happened or how he survived or ran some 6 or 7 miles home. Papa was born Aug. 4, 1873. He died June 30, 1963. I could tell you many more stories. I grew up & knew several of the survivors & witnesses. Plus, Papa was one of the many who helped dig the remains from the rubble. He didn't like to talk about that much…

Where I grew up the county roads are named for some of the elders. Marshall Cox road is one of those. Will McClelland Road is another. Another fact... the house Judson Woolley ran to & eventually lived in till he died... I bought it & now own it. It was built in 1930. My great grandmother, Mary Sartain (McClelland) was born on that land in a small shack. She died when I was a baby. To hear my mother talk of her was precious. Mother used to talk of Mammy's sense of humor with great pride & how proud of me she was, because I was the first male child born in several generations. I guess carrying on a family name or growing an extra farm hand was a good thing (at least they didn't live to see I had grown up to be a rock singer). There were many stories from those days. Mother's best friend (Donna) was married to Preston Crim. Preston was also a survivor from that day. He had jumped out a 2-story window and ran after watching his girlfriend's head cut off by some form of concrete slab. The teacher had told everyone to get under their desk when the rumbling started. His girlfriend was in plain sight of him. He only talked about it once to me, and I knew him for many years. Funny, so many people seem to want to know all the facts now... people who weren't there. But the people who were that I knew never wanted to talk about it and would go out of their way to avoid it. I found the people who would talk about it the most were like my family... ones that watched it go up, but weren't in it and didn't lose any of their loved ones. Papa didn't talk about his experience that I remember; Mother and Grandmother told me about it. Papa was a strong person, knowing his history and the things he had been through. Mother, being only four and living through it, had family come over all the time when she was growing up and want to do things with her and take her places, because they said she reminded them so much of their little girl that they lost. I was born in '53, but for many years of my youth, the disaster was still the most talked about subject in my house some 20 or 30 years later... I guess because so many who were there never got it out of their mind. They still have the sympathy letter here that they received from Hitler & various world leaders at the time.

Excerpts from 'A Reporter's Life'
by Walter Cronkite

I was sent to Dallas to temporarily relieve a personnel shortage. I had been there only a couple of days when the New London school in East Texas blew up. I was the editor of the state wire, and it was just coming upon three o'clock, when the wire was to be closed down for the night. Three bells rang on the machine and a coded message came across from Houston. The code was simple, but I hadn't had much reason to use it in my Kansas City duties, so, rather than take time to translate it right then, I went ahead with the procedure for closing down the wire. Now the bell rang frantically and, in the clear, came a message from Houston: "Don't close this wire!" That's what the coded message had said, too, and the reason became obvious within a minute or two.

Houston filed the first bulletin reporting that oil field sources had said there had been an explosion in the consolidated school at New London and requesting all the ambulances the area could send. The Dallas bureau manager and I took off immediately for New London, a good four hours away. We had to find it on the map, but our only delay was a slight detour so he could visit his bootlegger… We had no idea how bad the explosion had been until we reached Tyler, twenty-five miles from New

London. There was a funeral home on the main road, and for blocks around it there were ambulances and hearses and pickup trucks, all unloading bodies.

We hurried on to New London. We reached it just at dusk. Huge floodlights from the oil fields illuminated a great pile of rubble at which men and women tore with their bare hands. Many were workers from the oil fields, but among them were office workers and what appeared to be housewives. Many were parents, other volunteers, searching desperately for children still buried in the debris. Before they were through, they would bring 294 shattered, crushed bodies out of what had once been a two-story building, only four years old and considered one of the most up-to-date school structures in Texas.

The architect had reinforced the building with vertical rows of tiles. The building was heated with residual gas from the oil fields, gas so volatile and unstable that it is usually burned off in the flares we see around most oil fields. The gas is odorless and invisible. It leaked somewhere in the subbasement of the school building. It filled those vertical columns of tiles.

The school was a bomb waiting to explode. Two minutes before classes were to be dismissed for the weekend, a student in the basement woodworking shop switched off a band saw. The spark did its work.

To add to the horror, the Parent-Teacher Association was meeting in the school's gymnasium, just yards away. The mothers were there from the start of the frantic search for the few survivors. When we got there, the school superintendent, William Shaw, superficial cuts from the explosion bleeding across his face, was still wandering through the ruins. "There are children in there, there are children in there," he kept muttering. His own seventeen-year-old son was somewhere under the debris with two of his cousins.

A news reporter's duty can sometimes be difficult. It is not easy to approach someone in such distress to seek answers to the questions that need asking. Accuracy of a story is in direct relation to how soon after the event it is recorded, and how frequently the story has been retold.

Thus, I talked to the superintendent. I didn't know about the school's use of the highly dangerous residual gas. But he told me about it. He wept as he told how he and the school board had decided to tap into those gas lines. The use of the gas was illegal, but nearly everybody in the small towns adjoining the oil fields did it. The New London school simply was terribly unlucky. On one tottering wall a blackboard carried an ironic message: "Oil and natural gas are East Texas' greatest mineral blessings. Without them this school would not be here and none of us would be here learning our lessons." The world press poured into the little town of New London and its slightly larger neighbor, Overton.

"Carolyn's Speech"

One week after the tragedy on March 25, 1937, nine-year-old Carolyn Jones gave the following speech to the Texas legislature. This is the complete transcript of her speech:

Mr. President, members of the house of representatives, and friends of school children, I'm here today as a representative of the London School and as a survivor of the school explosion that took the lives of nearly 500 pupils, teachers, and parents.

Last Thursday afternoon while my colleague and I were studying spelling for the interscholastic meet in which we were going to represent our school the next day, our teacher Mrs. Sory saw some pictures fall from the wall and several vases crash from the desk.

In an instant she had jerked open two nearby windows and said, 'GET OUT OF HERE !!!' We were clinging to her when we heard the first awful rumble that in a few seconds caused the room to collapse.

Mrs. Sory helped us out of the window and in another few seconds we were separated by the dark cloud of dust that blinded us.

When it got so I could see again I ran home as fast as I could. My teacher and friend were not killed, but I did not see them again.

My sister Helen Jones, an honor student and member of the high school champion debate team, was not so fortunate. She and my uncle, Paul Grier, a senior who planned to study medicine, were both taken from us in this awful explosion that killed so many of the future generation of East Texas.

When the announcement was made a few hours earlier by our principle that school would be dismissed for the county meet, the usual joy and excitement of a holiday prevailed. Little did we realize that we soon would be searching in the ruins of our beautiful school building for the bodies of our sisters and brothers and teachers.

First, as a representative of these school friends and teachers of mine, both living and dead, I am here today to express our appreciation for all that you and our governor have done for the relief of the suffering people of this community.

Second, let us suggest the legislature of Texas set aside a special day each year to be observed as a memorial day on which tribute will be paid to the children and teachers who died in this catastrophe.

We want to thank you for the memorial fund to which many

of you have already contributed and which people all over the world are sending donations. We believe if those students and teachers who died would speak they would want a living memorial instead of a stately building.

By all means, we should have an appropriate but simple structure on which will appear the names of each pupil, teacher, and parent who died. With the remaining portion of money, our teachers suggest an endowment fund, to be used for the future education for the surviving children so that each might be assured of a college education if they so desired.

In conclusion, let me urge you, our lawmaking body, to make laws of safety, so it will not be possible for another explosion of this type to occur in the history of Texas schools.

Our daddies and mothers, as well as the teachers, want to know that when we leave our homes in the morning to go to school, that we will come out safe when our lessons are over.

Out of this explosion, we have learned of a new hazard that hovers about some of our school buildings. If this hazard can be forever blotted out of existence then we will not have completely lost our loved ones in vain.

We need say nothing more on the point of safety legislation because we as children of London school know that our faith *in our government will not be betrayed. We will have safe school buildings in the future.*

All of us who were spared will try to show our appreciation by striving to become the finest of citizens to carry on the work of this wonderful land of yours and mine.

This is our plea,

Thank you.

LESSONS OF THE 1937 TEXAS SCHOOL EXPLOSION

At the 2005 Reunion of the New London School Explosion, Carolyn Jones Frei again read her speech that she gave to the Texas legislature on March 25, 1937 as a fifth grader. She was standing in a corner of the London Museum. At her side was the machine that adds mercaptan, the warning smell to natural gas. Her speech inspired Ellie Goldberg to create "Lessons of the 1937 Texas School Explosion," a project dedicated to observing March 18th as an annual day to tell the story of the 1937 school tragedy and to promote leadership and partnerships to bring 'safety' from the margins to the core of school curriculum and community culture.

The goal of this project is to strengthen parent involvement and community partnerships to establish 21st century standards and safeguards that can protect children from deadly explosions, fires, chemical spills and toxic exposures.

Let us... set aside a special day each year to be observed as a memorial day on which tribute will be paid to the children and teachers who died in this catastrophe... and to make laws of safety... Our daddies and mothers, as well as the teachers, want to know that when we leave our homes in the morning to go to school, that we will come out safe when our lessons are over. --Carolyn Jones Frei

For more information about Lessons of the 1937 Texas School Explosion go to:

http://lessonsofthe1937texasschoolexplosion.blogspot.com

A Final Comment

Some mass disasters, like the one described in this book, take place suddenly and dramatically. Historical records are replete with multiple incidents of epic proportion, many reporting greater numbers of injuries and fatalities than that of the London School explosion of 1937. Often the lives of children have been involved, as well. However, it is the subtle, seemingly less consequential tragedies that find us at a loss at times when individuals or whole families are affected. Usually, not as many die so suddenly.

It is admittedly difficult not to become numb to the suffering of individuals and families who grieve for their loved ones on our daily news broadcasts. However, they still grieve in the same way those families mourned the loss of their children in New London, Texas seventy-five years ago. I am referring to killers like disease and vehicle accidents. Such are the deadly killers that swim with us daily in the murky ponds of our society. In 2008 motor vehicle traffic deaths in the U.S. reached over 42,000 individuals. One could argue, *What then are a mere 311, who died decades ago, in comparison?* One can indeed find logical justification for such an argument.

Improvements in vehicle and highway safety rates for 2011

are projected to be the lowest since 1949 levels, when more than 30,000 were killed on the America's roads and highways. If future projections are realized, tens of thousands will be saved in future years compared to the past. By doing what is needed, lives can indeed be saved. Such statistics of lives lost and broken are staggering when compared to most major disasters of any kind.

According to the U.S. Fire and Explosion Statistics, during the three-year period from 2003 to 2006, fire departments responded to an estimated 2,400 home fires caused by gasoline. From 2000 to 2004, an estimated 3,800 home fires resulted from gas fuel ignition. In 2004 alone, 148 people died from gas and other explosions. In just one year, in 2006, home heating equipment was involved in an estimated 64,000 home fires that caused 540 related deaths and 1,400 injuries. Fires caused 3,320 civilian deaths and 16,705 injuries in 2008. Single disasters pale in comparison.

One of the most tragic realities of our modern age is a statistically limited opportunity for our children to survive into adulthood. Our duty, as citizens who genuinely care for our families and neighbors, is to do whatever each of us can, individually and as groups, to increase their safety and minimize future suffering for everyone. If a time comes for you to make a sacrifice (either small or great) that may one day save the life of a child, I hope you will do the right thing and remember that they are the hope that lies within us. Without the children, our light cannot shine.

I have decided to close this book with the familiar lyrics of this ever-popular song that often reverberated in my own mind while writing this book. It was written in 1910 by Frederic Weatherly and never fails to bring a tear to my eyes.

Danny Boy

Oh Danny Boy, the pipes, the pipes are calling
From glen to glen, and down the mountain side
The summer's gone, and all the flowers are dying
'Tis you, 'tis you ...must go and I must bide.

But come ye back when summer's in the meadow
Or when the valley's hushed and white with snow
'Tis I'll be here in sunshine or in shadow
Oh Danny Boy, oh Danny Boy, I love you so.

And if you come, when all the flowers are dying
And I am dead, as dead I well may be
You'll come and find the place where I am lying
And kneel and say an "Ave" there for me.

And I shall hear, tho' soft you tread above me
And all my dreams will warm and sweeter be
If you'll not fail to tell me that you love me
I'll simply sleep in peace until you come to me.

Oh, Danny Boy, Oh, Danny Boy, I love you so.

References:

http://www.newlondonschool.org/
http://www.frontporchnewstexas.com/newlondonschool.htm
http://en.wikipedia.org/wiki/New_London_School_explosion
http://www.hilliard.ws/nlondon.htm
http://www.dallasobserver.com/2002-02-21/news/today-a-generatio
n-died/
http://www.depotmuseum.com/newLondon.html
http://www.southlakeenergy.com/education/east-texas-history/
http://www.titushistory.com/business_oil_grow_01.html
http://www.old-time.com/halper/halper37.html
http://www.localnewsonly.com/areanews/03mar15newlondon.htm
http://www.texasescapes.com/AllThingsHistorical/New-London-Mu
seum-BB305.htm
http://www.carthagetexas.com/Center/stories/school_explosion.htm
http://www.texas-fire.com/2007/03/anniversary-of-1937-new-londo
n-explosion
http://www.kuhf.org/site/News2?page=NewsArticle&id=22755
http://www.suite101.com/content/walter-cronkite-the-most-trusted-
man-in-american-journalism-a337476
http://articles.latimes.com/1987-03-22/news/mn-14795_1_natural-g
as-leak
http://www.jomirabooks.com/artwork/newlondon.html
http://www.wfaa.com/home/Worst-Texas-school-disaster-passes-73
rd-anniversary-88723767.html
http://www.voluntaryist.com/articles/119a.html
http://www.explosionattorneys.com/fire-explosion-statistics.html
http://www.suite101.com/content/new-london-school-disaster-wors
t-ever-in-us-a127067

http://overtontx.com/2010/03/20/claude-kerce-new-london-survivio
r/
www.nfpa.org/assets/files//PDF/London_Texas_School_1937.pdf
http://www.funeralhelper.org/the-rose-beyond-the-wall-a-l-frink-po
pular.html
http://www.kristinbeauchamp.com

"Where Even Angels Wept" documentary:
http://www.youtube.com/watch?v=jf2OwBvdKEk

Related videos:
http://www.youtube.com/watch?v=GEz9B_GUsmg
http://en.wikipedia.org/wiki/File:New_London_school_explosion_of
_1937_newsreel.ogv
http://www.c-spanvideo.org/videoLibrary/clip.php?appid=59522357
4
http://www.youtube.com/watch?v=aKt01p3DJRw
http://www.cbs19.tv/story/14285302/survivors-alumni-remember-lo
ndon-school-explosion?redirected=true
http://www.youtube.com/watch?v=1osJ1dUvwco

Thank you for taking the time to read
An Empty Tomb Where Roses Bloom
If you enjoyed it, please recommend it to others.

To obtain a free PDF download of this or any of my other books,
simply rate and review this book at the site where it was obtained.

Then, just send a message requesting the free book you want at
http://www.facebook.com/KerryL.Barger .

To the Reader:

*"**Lest we never forget...**"* September 11th will undoubtedly be recognized and passed into law as a national holiday in the near future.

March 18th should be recognized and passed into law as a state holiday in Texas *"...so future generations will always remember!"*

If you agree, I urge you to contact your county and state representative/s and ask them to begin promoting legislation to this effect immediately.

Thank you,
Kerry L. Barger

11763185R00127

Made in the USA
Charleston, SC
19 March 2012